# The Usborne
# Children's
# Cookbook

Rebecca Gilpin

Designed by Non Figg and Nancy Leschnikoff
Illustrated by Molly Sage and Adam Larkum

Photography by Howard Allman
Recipes and food preparation by Catherine Atkinson

American expert: Barbara Tricinella    American editor: Carrie Armstrong

# Contents

# Using this book

The delicious recipes in this book are ideal for anyone who is just starting out in the kitchen. The recipes are explained in a clear, simple way, without baffling cooking terms and jargon. As well as the recipes, there are general pages that show you how to cook things such as rice, potatoes and bread rolls. You'll also find helpful chefs who give you cooking tips and hints. So, read this page, then get cooking!

## Getting ready

Before you start, check that you've got all the ingredients that are in the list at the beginning of the recipe. Read through the recipe too, to make sure that you have all the equipment you will need.

## The right amount

When you add a spoonful of something to a mixture, the ingredient should lie level with the top of the spoon and not heaped up. Measuring spoons found in a set are the easiest to use, but if you don't have any, use ordinary spoons.

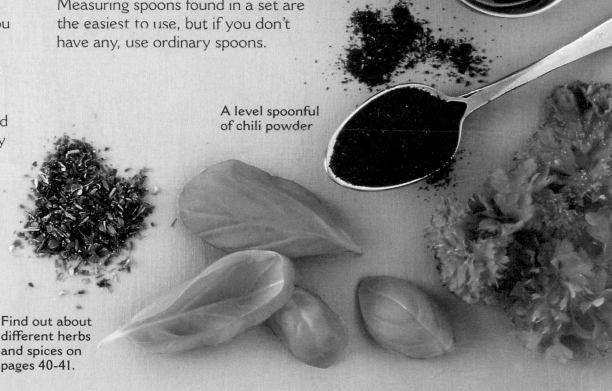

A set of measuring spoons

A level spoonful of chili powder

## Cooking times

Not all ovens are the same and some cook things more quickly or slowly. Check to see if the food is cooked, close to the cooking time in the recipe.

Find out about different herbs and spices on pages 40-41.

## Salt and pepper

In the recipes, salt and pepper are added a pinch at a time. A 'pinch' is the amount you can pick up between your first finger and thumb. Don't add more than it says – you can add extra when you eat the food.

## Hot ovens

When you're cooking something in an oven, put it on the middle shelf unless the recipe says something else. Fan ovens are hotter than other ovens, so check in the instruction book to see if you need to lower the temperature or cook something for less time.

## Serving suggestions

Some of the recipes in this book are complete meals in themselves. Other recipes have suggestions for things that could be served with them. If you want to serve something with potatoes, rice or a salad, look in the index at the back of the book.

# Greek salad

Greek salad is great as a summer lunch, served with fresh crusty bread. It contains feta, a white salty Greek cheese, as well as cucumber, tomatoes, onions and olives.

## Ingredients:

Serves 4

half a cucumber
1 lb. ripe tomatoes
1 red onion
7 oz. package of feta cheese
3 oz. pitted black or green
    olives, drained

For the dressing:
1 garlic clove
4 tablespoons olive oil
1 tablespoon white wine vinegar
½ teaspoon fresh or
    ¼ teaspoon dried oregano
a pinch of granulated sugar
salt and ground black pepper

## Chef's Tip

Olives can be very salty. If you want to make them less salty, soak them in cold water for an hour, then drain them through a colander.

If the cucumber has a waxy skin, peel it with a potato peeler.

1. Cut the ends off the cucumber, then cut it in half along its length. Lay each half with the flat side facing down. Then, cut both halves into thin slices.

Core

2. Cut the tomatoes into quarters. Then, carefully cut out the central core of each one and throw it away. Put the tomato quarters and cucumber slices into a large bowl.

3. Cut the ends off the onion. Peel it and cut it into quarters, then cut the quarters into slices. Then, put the feta cheese onto the cutting board, too.

4. Cut the cheese into cubes, then add it to the bowl. Add the slices of onion and most of the olives. Mix everything together with your hands.

You need to use a jar with a lid.

5. Peel and crush the garlic. Put the olive oil, vinegar, garlic, oregano and sugar into a jar. Add a pinch of salt and of pepper, then screw the lid on tightly.

6. Shake the jar well to mix the dressing. Drizzle the dressing over the salad, then mix it with your hands. Then, scatter the rest of the olives over the top.

# Couscous salad

Couscous is often eaten with grilled meat, fish or vegetables. It can also be mixed with other ingredients to make a salad. This recipe has a fresh lemon juice dressing.

## Ingredients:

Serves 4

8 green onions
half a bouillon cube
1 tablespoon sunflower oil
1 cup couscous
4 ripe tomatoes
half a cucumber
1 yellow pepper
4 tablespoons chopped fresh mint

For the dressing:
2 tablespoons sunflower oil
2 tablespoons fresh lemon juice
salt and ground black pepper

## Chef's Tip

Bouillon is used to add flavor to recipes, but it's not a problem here if you don't have any. You can cook the couscous in boiling water instead.

1. Using a sharp knife, cut off the ends of the green onions and remove the outer layer. Then, cut the onions into diagonal slices about ½ inch wide.

Cook on medium heat.

3. Put one tablespoon of oil in a large saucepan and add the onions. Heat the pan for 30 seconds, then pour in the broth. Cook the mixture until the liquid boils.

5. If there is still any liquid in the pan, gently heat it over low heat for a few minutes, until all the liquid is absorbed. Keep stirring the couscous to stop it from sticking.

2. Put the half bouillon cube into a heatproof container. Then, pour in 1 cup of boiling water and stir it until the bouillon cube has completely dissolved.

4. Remove the pan from the heat and add the couscous. Stir it in with a wooden spoon. Then, cover the pan with a lid and leave it for three minutes.

6. For the dressing, put two tablespoons of oil in a small bowl. Add the lemon juice and a pinch of salt and of pepper and mix everything with a fork.

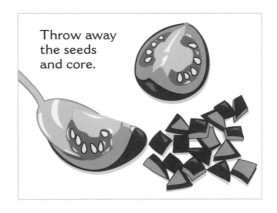

Throw away the seeds and core.

You don't need the seeds.

If the cucumber has a waxy skin, peel it with a potato peeler.

7. Spoon the couscous into a large bowl. While it is still warm, pour the dressing over it. Use a fork to break up any lumps, then leave the couscous to cool.

8. Cut the tomatoes in half and then in half again. Scoop out the seeds with a teaspoon. Then, cut out the green core and cut the tomatoes into small pieces.

9. Cut the ends off the cucumber and cut it in half, lengthways. Scoop out the seeds, then cut each half into long strips. Then, cut each strip into small pieces.

You could serve the couscous on some mixed salad leaves.

10. Cut the ends off the yellow pepper and cut it in half. Remove the seeds and cut the pepper into small pieces. Then, mix the mint and vegetables into the couscous.

# Potato salad and green salad

Potatoes can be eaten hot or cold. This potato salad can be eaten while it's still warm but is also good served chilled, with a crunchy green salad and lamb kebabs (see pages 58-59).

## Ingredients:

Serves 4

1½ lbs. equal-sized new potatoes
salt
4 green onions

For the dressing:
3 tablespoons mayonnaise
3 tablespoons plain
    non-fat yogurt
1 teaspoon fresh lemon juice
1 teaspoon wholegrain (spicy)
    mustard
2 tablespoons chopped fresh dill
a pinch of freshly ground black
    pepper

For the green salad:
crisp lettuce leaves
half a cucumber
1 green pepper

## Chef's Tip

If some of your new potatoes are much bigger than the others, cut them in half. All the pieces need to be about the same size, so that they cook in the same time.

Scrub the potatoes under cold water.

1. Scrub the potatoes clean with a soft brush. Then, half-fill a large saucepan with water and add two pinches of salt. Heat the water until it boils.

3. While the potatoes are cooking, put all the ingredients for the dressing into a small bowl. Then, stir them with a spoon until they are mixed together.

5. Using a sharp knife, cut off the ends of the green onions, and remove the outer layer. Then, cut across the onions to make lots of thin slices, like this.

2. Put the potatoes into the pan. Heat the water until it boils, then reduce the heat a little, so that the water is gently bubbling. Cook the potatoes for 15-20 minutes.

4. Put a colander in the sink and carefully pour the cooked potatoes into it. Shake the colander a little, to drain off any extra water. Then, leave the potatoes to cool a little.

6. When the potatoes are cool enough to handle, put them on a cutting board and cut them into bite-sized pieces. Then, put all the pieces into a large bowl.

Take
out the
seeds, too.

If the cucumber has a
waxy skin, peel it
with a peeler.

7. Spoon the dressing over the potatoes while they are still slightly warm. Add the slices of green onion and mix everything together with a large spoon.

8. For the green salad, cut off the bottom of the lettuce and remove some leaves. Wash them and shake them dry. Then, cut the ends off the pepper and finely slice it.

9. Cut the ends off the cucumber, then cut it in half, lengthways. Cut each half into lots of thin slices, then put the lettuce, pepper and cucumber into a large bowl.

You could dress the green salad with French dressing (see steps 11 and 12 on page 17).

Let the potato salad cool completely and keep it in the refrigerator until you're ready to eat it.

Sprinkle chopped green onions on top and add a sprig of dill.

# Potato soup

This soup can make a warming meal on a winter day, but it's also delicious cold. The recipe uses a food processor, but if you cut the vegetables into very small pieces, you can make a chunky soup instead. If you use leeks and have never prepared them before, look at page 53 before you start.

## Ingredients:

Serves 4

3 leeks or 4 large green onions
1 onion
3 tablespoons butter
about 3 medium potatoes
1 vegetable bouillon cube
1 bay leaf
salt and ground black pepper
½ cup milk

## Chef's Tip

If you pour hot soup straight from the pan into a bowl, you may get splashed. It's much safer to spoon the soup into the bowl using a ladle.

1. Trim the leeks or green onions, then slice them. Cut the ends off the onion and peel it. Cut it in half, slice it and cut it into small pieces. Put the butter into a large pan.

Steam escapes through the gap.

2. Gently heat the butter until it melts. Stir in the leeks or green onions, and onion, to coat them with melted butter. Put a lid on the pan, leaving a small gap.

Put the lid back on when you've stirred the soup.

3. Cook the leeks and onion on low heat for 8-10 minutes, stirring them every now and then, with a wooden spoon. When they are soft, turn off the heat.

4. Peel the potatoes and cut them in half. Cut the halves into slices and cut the slices into small chunks. Then, put the bouillon cube in a heatproof container.

5. Pour 2 cups of boiling water into the container and stir it until the bouillon cube has dissolved. Then, add the broth and the chunks of potato to the pan.

6. Add the bay leaf and a pinch of salt and of pepper. Heat the soup until it boils, then turn down the heat, so that it is gently bubbling. Cover the pan with a lid, as before.

Press a wooden spoon against the potatoes to check that they are soft.

7. Cook the soup for 15-20 minutes, or until the potatoes are soft. Turn off the heat and remove the bay leaf with a spoon. Then, let the soup cool for 15 minutes.

Stir in a spoonful of sour cream and grated Cheddar cheese. Sprinkle chopped chives on top.

8. Ladle half of the soup into a food processor and blend it until it is smooth. Spoon it into a large bowl, then blend the rest. Pour all of the soup back into the pan.

9. Add the milk and stir it in. For hot soup, gently reheat the soup until it is just starting to bubble. Alternatively, for cold soup, put the soup in a refrigerator to chill.

# Spicy bean soup

This soup is hot and spicy. If you'd like it to be less spicy, just add the coriander and cumin and leave out the chili powder.

## Ingredients:

Serves 4

1 red onion
1 tablespoon olive oil
1 vegetable bouillon cube
1 clove of garlic
½ teaspoon mild chili powder
½ teaspoon ground coriander
½ teaspoon ground cumin
1½ cups tomato juice
salt and ground black pepper
14 oz. can red kidney beans
   or mixed beans
1 tablespoon chopped fresh
   coriander or parsley

1. Peel the onion and cut it in half. Finely slice it, then cut all of the slices into small pieces. Put the pieces of onion into a large saucepan with the olive oil.

2. Heat the pan on low heat and gently cook the onion for 6-10 minutes, until it is soft. Stir the onion frequently, to keep it from sticking to the pan.

You could sprinkle each bowl with chopped fresh coriander or parsley.

If you want to make bread rolls to eat with your soup, see pages 74-75.

3. While the onion is cooking, put the bouillon cube into a heatproof container. Carefully pour 1½ cups of boiling water into the container and stir it until the cube dissolves.

4. Take the pan off the heat. Peel and crush the garlic and add it to the pan. Then, add the chili powder, ground coriander and ground cumin, too.

5. Stir everything in the pan together. Then, heat the pan gently for one minute, stirring all the time, to keep the spices from sticking as they cook.

## Chef's Tip

6. Pour the tomato juice and broth into the pan and add a pinch of salt and of pepper. Open the can of beans and pour them into a colander in the sink.

Cans of beans usually contain a sugary liquid, as well as the beans. To rinse off the liquid, hold the colander under cold running water and gently shake the beans.

7. Add the rinsed beans to the pan. Stir the soup well and heat it until it boils. Then, reduce the heat a little, so that the soup is gently bubbling.

Steam escapes through the gap.

Scoop up lots of beans with the ladle, too.

8. Put the lid on the pan, leaving a small gap. Cook the soup for 15 minutes, stirring it from time to time. Then, turn off the heat and let the soup cool for 15 minutes.

9. Using a ladle, put half of the soup into a food processor and blend it until it is smooth and thick. Then, ladle the blended soup back into the pan.

10. Stir all of the soup in the pan together, then heat it until it is gently bubbling. Stir in the chopped coriander or parsley, then serve the soup.

# Eggs

Eggs are used in many recipes, but they can also be cooked by themselves. On these pages, you can find out how to prepare them for use in recipes, and how to boil, hard-boil and fry them.

Break eggs into a separate bowl or cup before adding them to a mixture (see left).

## Separate bowls

Make sure that the eggs you're using are fresh. In case they're not, it's a good idea to break them into a separate bowl or cup before you add them to a mixture. This means that you can throw away an egg that has gone bad without having to throw everything else away too. In some recipes you may need only the egg white or yolk, so you'll need to separate the egg (see below).

## Breaking an egg

1. Unless you're boiling an egg, you'll need to break its shell. Crack the shell, by tapping it sharply on the edge of a bowl or cup.

2. Push your thumbs into the crack and pull the shell apart. Slide the egg into the bowl or cup and check for pieces of shell.

## Separating

Break an egg onto a plate. Cover the yolk with a cup, then hold the cup and tip the plate. The egg white slides off.

## Beating

When you beat an egg, you need to mix the yolk and the white of the egg evenly. Use a fork to mix them together.

## Whisking egg whites

The dish towel helps to keep the bowl from slipping.

1. Separate the eggs, then pour the whites into a clean, dry bowl. Place the bowl on a damp dish towel, then tilt the bowl.

Use a clean whisk.

2. Using your other hand, twist a whisk around and around very quickly in the bowl. The egg will begin to go white and frothy.

3. Continue whisking the eggs until stiff points or 'peaks' form on the top when you lift up the whisk, like this.

## Boiling an egg

For a solid yolk, cook the egg for longer.

Heat a pan of water until the water is boiling. Then, put an egg into the pan, using a spoon. Boil the egg for 4 minutes.

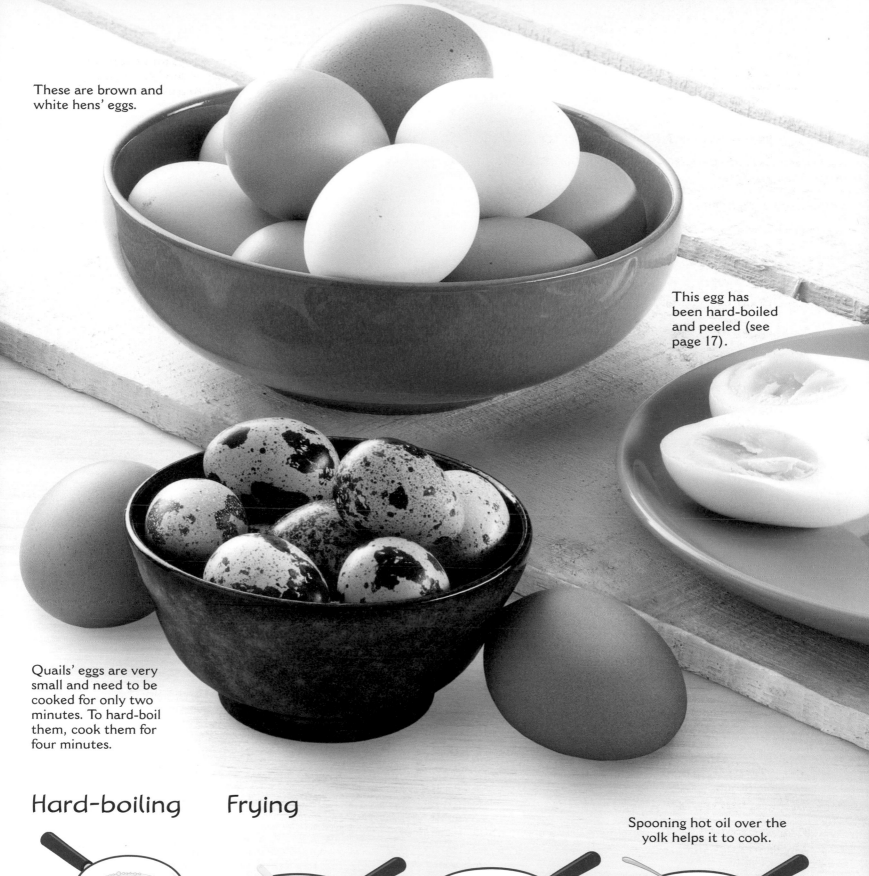

These are brown and white hens' eggs.

This egg has been hard-boiled and peeled (see page 17).

Quails' eggs are very small and need to be cooked for only two minutes. To hard-boil them, cook them for four minutes.

## Hard-boiling

For a hard-boiled egg, boil the egg for 10 minutes, then lift it out and place it in a bowl of cold water, to cool.

## Frying

Spooning hot oil over the yolk helps it to cook.

1. Pour a tablespoon of vegetable oil into a frying pan. Heat the pan on medium heat for a minute, then take it off the heat.

2. Crack an egg, then hold it just above the pan and open the shell. Pour the egg into the oil, then put the pan on the heat.

3. When the egg white starts to turn solid, spoon hot oil over the yolk. Fry the egg for 3-4 minutes, until it is cooked.

15

# Salade niçoise

This salad is delicious and filling. It was first made in Nice, in the south of France, using local ingredients such as olives, anchovies and tuna.

## Ingredients:

Serves 4

2 medium eggs
1 lb. small new potatoes
8 oz. thin green beans
crisp lettuce leaves
1 red onion
half a cucumber
16 ripe cherry tomatoes
2 oz. can anchovies
7 oz. can tuna in oil
12 pitted black olives
2 teaspoons capers (optional)

For the French dressing:
4 tablespoons olive oil
1 tablespoon balsamic vinegar,
   or red wine vinegar
½ teaspoon Dijon mustard
salt and ground black pepper

1. Hard-boil the eggs (see page 15). Then, scrub the potatoes clean with a brush, in cold water. Half-fill a large saucepan with water and heat it until the water boils.

2. Using a spoon, put the potatoes in the pan. Heat the water until it boils. Reduce the heat a little so that the water is gently bubbling. Cook the potatoes for 10 minutes.

Use clean kitchen scissors.

3. While the potatoes cook, cut off the ends of the beans, then cut them in half. When the potatoes have been cooking for 10 minutes, add the beans to the pan.

4. Bring the water back to a boil and cook the potatoes and beans for five minutes. Put a colander into the sink and carefully pour the vegetables into it.

You could serve the salad with freshly-baked bread rolls (see pages 74-75).

The pieces should be bite-sized.

If the cucumber has a waxy skin, peel it with a potato peeler.

5. When the potatoes are cool enough to handle, cut each one in half. Then, put the potatoes and beans in a large bowl and leave them to cool.

6. Cut off the bottom of the lettuce and remove some leaves. Wash them well in cold water. Shake them dry, then break the leaves into pieces.

7. Cut the ends off the onion and peel it. Then, cut it into halves and slice it. Cut off the ends of the cucumber, then cut it into slices. Then, cut the tomatoes in half.

## Chef's Tip

Cut them from top to bottom.

Don't rinse the tuna.

8. Carefully open the can of anchovies and pour them into a sieve. They are very salty, so rinse them with cold tap water. Then, cut each one in half.

9. Open the can of tuna and drain off the oil. Break it into large chunks. Add it to the bowl, with the anchovies, cucumber, lettuce, onion and tomatoes.

In the next step, you'll be peeling the shells off the hard-boiled eggs. Tap each egg gently on a plate until the shell cracks all the way around, then peel off the pieces.

Cut the eggs lengthways.

10. Peel the shells off the eggs and cut each egg into quarters. Then, drain the olives through a sieve. If you are using capers, spoon them into the sieve and drain them too.

11. Add the eggs, olives and capers to the bowl. Then, for the dressing, put the olive oil, vinegar, mustard and a pinch of salt and of pepper into a glass jar with a lid.

12. Screw the lid onto the jar, then shake the jar to mix the ingredients. Pour the dressing over the salad. Mix everything well with a large spoon.

# Spanish omelette

This tasty vegetarian omelette is packed with vegetables. It is light and fluffy, but filling, too. Some omelettes are cooked in a frying pan, but this one is baked in the oven. It can be eaten right away or when it has cooled.

## Ingredients:

Serves 4

1 onion
2 medium-sized potatoes
1 zucchini
1 clove of garlic
2 tablespoons olive oil
1 tablespoon butter
5 medium eggs
½ cup milk
½ teaspoon of seasoning
salt and ground black pepper

a shallow 8-9 inch ovenproof dish

1. Preheat the oven to 350°F. While it is heating up, wipe a paper towel in a little butter, then wipe butter over the inside of the dish.

2. Cut the ends off the onion and peel it. Cut it in half, then into thin slices. Then, peel the potatoes and cut them in half. Cut them into thin slices and then into cubes.

3. Cut the ends off the zucchini and cut it in half lengthways. Cut the halves into strips and cut the strips into small pieces. Then, peel the clove of garlic.

Stir the onion and potatoes now and then.

4. Put the oil and butter into a non-stick frying pan. Heat them on a low heat until the butter melts. Add the onion and potatoes and cook them for five minutes.

Stir the vegetables often.

5. Add the pieces of zucchini and crush the garlic into the pan. Cook everything gently for another five minutes, or until the vegetables are slightly soft.

6. Take the pan off the heat and spoon the vegetables into the ovenproof dish. Spread them out to make an even layer. Then, break the eggs into a large bowl.

7. Beat the eggs with a fork, then pour in the milk. Add the seasoning and a pinch of salt and of pepper. Then, beat everything together until they are mixed well.

The omelette is delicious served with mixed salad leaves or a green salad like the one on pages 8-9.

8. Pour the egg mixture over the vegetables. Then, put the dish into the oven and bake the omelette for 40 minutes, until it is set and golden brown.

Lift out the pieces with a spatula or pie slice.

9. Push a knife into the middle of the omelette. If runny egg comes out, cook it for 5-10 minutes more. Then, run a knife around the edge and cut the omelette into pieces.

# Croque-monsieur

This hot sandwich is perfect on its own as a light meal, or delicious served with a crunchy mixed salad.

## Ingredients:

Serves 4

4 oz. (1 cup) Cheddar cheese
8 slices bread
4 tablespoons butter, softened
4 slices of lean ham
2 teaspoons sunflower oil

For the mixed salad:
crispy lettuce leaves
half a cucumber
1 carrot

Sprinkle the cheese as evenly as you can.

1. Lay four of the slices of bread on a cutting board. Spread a thin layer of butter on one side of each one. Then, butter the other four slices of bread in the same way.

You could make the French dressing on pages 16-17 and sprinkle it over the salad.

2. Grate the cheese on the big holes on a grater. Then, sprinkle the grated cheese over four of the slices of buttered bread and lay a slice of ham on the top.

If the cucumber has a waxy skin, peel it with a potato peeler.

3. Gently press a slice of bread on top of each slice of ham. Cut each sandwich in half with a sharp knife, then put them on a plate and cover them with plastic foodwrap.

4. For the salad, cut the bottom off the lettuce. Pull off some leaves, rinse them in cold water and shake them dry. Tear them into bite-sized pieces and put them into a bowl.

5. Cut the ends off the cucumber. Then, cut the cucumber in half, lengthways, and in half again. Cut the pieces into small chunks, then add them to the bowl.

6. Peel the carrot with a potato peeler. Then, hold it firmly and carefully grate it on the biggest holes on a grater. Add the carrot to the bowl and mix everything well.

7. Put one teaspoon of the sunflower oil into a large, non-stick frying pan. Then, heat the oil over medium heat for about a minute.

## Chef's Tip

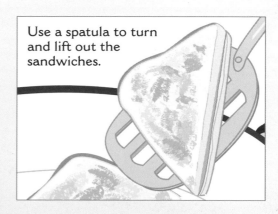

Use a spatula to turn and lift out the sandwiches.

8. Carefully put four of the half sandwiches into the frying pan. Cook them for 2-3 minutes, or until their undersides have turned brown and crisp.

When you fry things in a pan, they can cook very quickly. To see if the sandwiches are cooked, slide a spatula under a corner of one of them and take a look.

9. Turn the sandwiches over. Cook them for 2-3 minutes, then lift them out of the pan. Add another teaspoon of oil to the pan and cook the remaining sandwiches.

# Beefburgers with tomato salsa

These tasty beefburgers are baked in the oven. They are delicious served with fresh tomato salsa and chunky potato wedges (see page 65).

## Ingredients:

Serves 4

For the tomato salsa:
6 ripe tomatoes
1 red onion
2 tablespoons chopped fresh coriander
1 tablespoon olive oil
1 teaspoon balsamic vinegar or red wine vinegar
salt and ground black pepper

For the burgers:
1 tablespoon olive oil
1 teaspoon mixed seasoning
2 teaspoons soy sauce or Worcestershire sauce
1 slice white bread, with the crusts removed
1 medium egg
1 lb. extra-lean ground beef
salt and ground black pepper

1. Preheat the oven to 400°F. While it is heating up, put a teaspoon of cooking oil on a baking tray. Wipe the oil over the tray with a paper towel.

2. For the salsa, cut each tomato in half, then into quarters. Cut out the core of each one, like this. Throw away the cores, then cut all the quarters into small pieces.

Keep the other half of the onion for the burgers.

3. Peel the onion and chop it finely. Put half of it into a bowl with the tomatoes and add the chopped coriander, olive oil, vinegar and a pinch of salt and of pepper.

4. Stir everything in the bowl together, then put the salsa aside. Then, put the rest of the onion into a frying pan with a tablespoon of olive oil.

## Chef's Tip

5. Cook the onion on low heat for 8-10 minutes, stirring it frequently to keep it from sticking to the pan. When the onion is soft, take the pan off the heat.

6. Spoon the onion into a large bowl. Stir in the dried mixed herbs and soy or Worcestershire sauce and leave the mixture to cool for about 10 minutes.

In the next step, you'll be making breadcrumbs in a food processor. If you don't have one, grate some bread on the big holes on a grater. Slightly stale bread works best.

Use clean hands to mix the ingredients.

Leave spaces between the burgers.

7. Make the slices of bread into breadcrumbs, using a food processor (see page 94) or a grater. Then, break the egg into a small bowl and beat it with a fork.

8. Add the breadcrumbs, egg, beef and a pinch of salt and of pepper to the large bowl. Break up the beef with a wooden spoon, then mix all the ingredients together well.

9. Divide the mixture into four pieces. Make each piece into a circle about ½ inch thick. Then, put the burgers on the greased baking tray.

Turn the burgers with a spatula.

10. Cook the burgers in the oven for 10 minutes. Then, lift them out, wearing oven mitts. Turn the burgers over and cook them for another 10 minutes.

11. To check that the burgers are cooked all the way through, push a knife into them, then press on the top. The juices that run out should be clear, not pink.

23

# Pastry crust

On these pages, you can find out how to make shortcrust pastry, which is used to make flans, pies and quiches (see pages 26-27). You'll also find out how to 'blind' bake a pastry crust, before filling it. It's much easier to make a pastry crust if your hands are cool, but once you've made it, try not to handle it too much.

## 'Blind' baking

When a pastry crust is 'blind' baked, it is cooked for a time with no filling. It is lined with kitchen foil and filled with ceramic baking beans, or dried beans or peas, which keep the pastry from bubbling up in the middle.

If you use dried beans or peas when you're baking a pastry crust, store them in an airtight jar, so that you can use them again and again.

## Ingredients:

Makes enough pastry to line an 8 inch pie pan

1½ cup all-purpose flour
salt
6 tablespoons butter, or margarine from a stick
3-5 tablespoons cold water

baking beans, or a package of dried beans or peas

1. Sift the flour and a pinch of salt through a sieve into a large bowl. Then, cut the butter into cubes and stir them in.

2. Rub the butter into the flour with the tips of your fingers. Continue rubbing until the mixture looks like fine breadcrumbs.

Use a blunt knife.

3. Sprinkle three tablespoons of cold water over the mixture. Then, stir it in, until everything starts to stick together.

This pastry has been rolled out, which means that it has been rolled flat with a rolling pin.

4. If the dough feels dry, mix in another tablespoon or two of water. Then, squeeze the dough against the side of the bowl.

5. Sprinkle a little flour on a clean work surface. Then, lift the dough onto the surface and pat it into a smooth ball.

6. Wrap the dough in plastic foodwrap. Then, put it into the refrigerator for 20 minutes, to make it easier to roll out flat.

Ceramic baking beans, like these, can usually be bought in the cooking section of any large store.

## Lining a pastry crust

Turn the dough a quarter of the way around.

1. Put the dough onto a floury surface. Sprinkle flour on a rolling pin. Roll over the dough once, then turn it.

2. Roll over and turn the dough again and again. Continue until the dough is slightly bigger than the pie pan.

Be careful not to make any holes in the dough.

3. Roll the dough around the rolling pin. Lift it up and unroll it over the pan. Gently push the dough into the edges of the pan.

The rolling pin cuts off any extra dough.

4. Roll the rolling pin over the pan. Then, cover the pastry crust with plastic foodwrap and put it in the refrigerator for 20 minutes.

## 'Blind' baking

The holes stop the dough from rising up.

1. Put a baking sheet in the oven. Preheat the oven to 400°F. Then, prick the dough base with a fork.

Try not to squash the pastry.

2. Cut a large square of kitchen foil and gently press it into the dough. Then, fill the foil with baking beans.

3. Lift out the hot baking sheet and put the pie pan on it. Put it back into the oven and bake the crust for 10 minutes.

4. Carefully remove the hot foil and beans. Then, bake the empty crust for another 8-10 minutes, or until it is pale golden.

# Bacon and onion quiche

To make the pastry crust for this tasty quiche, you'll need to follow the steps on pages 24-25. When you've 'blind' baked the base, you can make the filling for the quiche.

## Ingredients:

Serves 4

For the crust:
1½ cups all-purpose flour
salt
6 tablespoons butter or margarine from a block
3-5 tablespoons cold water

For the filling:
6 strips Canadian bacon
1 onion
1 tablespoon sunflower oil
4 oz. (1 cup) Cheddar cheese
2 large eggs
½ cup milk
ground black pepper

baking beans or a package of dried peas or beans, for 'blind' baking
8 inch pie pan, about 1½ inches deep

Be very careful when you remove the hot foil and beans.

The hot baking sheet helps the bottom of the quiche to cook.

1. To make the pastry crust, follow the steps on pages 24-25. Line the pan with the dough, then 'blind' bake the dough. When it is cooked, take it out of the oven.

2. Put the hot baking sheet back into the oven on its own. Reduce the temperature of the oven to 325°F. Then, prepare the filling for the quiche.

3. If there is any rind on the bacon, cut it off with clean kitchen scissors and throw the rind away. Then, cut the rest of the bacon into small pieces.

4. Peel the onion and cut it in half. Slice it, then cut it into small pieces. Put the pieces into a frying pan with the oil and cook them gently for about five minutes.

5. Add the bacon to the pan and stir it in. Then, turn off the heat and pour the pieces of bacon and onion into a bowl. Let them cool for five minutes.

The quiche can be eaten hot, but it is also delicious chilled. Make sure it is completely cool before you put it in the refrigerator.

6. Grate the cheese on the large holes on a grater and sprinkle half of it over the bottom of the crust. Then, scatter the bacon and onion over the top.

7. Sprinkle over the rest of the cheese. Break the eggs into a bowl and mix them with a fork. Pour the milk into a container and mix in the egg and a pinch of pepper.

The top should be golden and the middle set firm.

8. Slowly pour the egg mixture over the filling in the crust. Then, carefully lift the hot baking sheet out of the oven and put the quiche onto it.

9. Bake the quiche for about 20-30 minutes, then push a knife into the middle. If it isn't firm, cook it for 5-10 minutes more. Leave it in the pan for 10 minutes before serving it.

# Pizza

This pizza has a light bread crust, topped with a tasty tomato sauce and grated mozzarella. It takes a little while to make the crust, but it's delicious.

## Ingredients:

Serves 4

For the crust:
1¾ cup white bread flour
½ teaspoon of salt
1 teaspoon rapid-rise yeast
   (½ package)
1 teaspoon sugar
½ cup warm water
1 tablespoon olive oil

For the tomato sauce:
two cloves of garlic
1 tablespoon olive oil
14 oz. can chopped tomatoes
a pinch of sugar
½ teaspoon dried oregano
salt and ground black pepper

For the topping:
1¼ cups ready-grated
   mozzarella or 'pizza' cheese
2 oz. pepperoni or ham
15-16 pitted black olives

## Chef's Tip

You can add all kinds of toppings to pizzas – try pepperoni and onion, or ham and pineapple, or top a pizza with stir-fried vegetables (see pages 38-39).

1. To make the bread dough for the crust, follow steps 1-5 on pages 74-75. When you have put it in a warm place to rise, you can start to make the tomato sauce.

Stir the sauce often, to keep it from sticking.

3. Heat the sauce on medium heat, stirring it often, for about 15 minutes or until it is really thick. Then, take the pan off the heat and leave the sauce to cool.

5. Put the dough back into the mixing bowl and leave it in a warm place to rise again for about 40 minutes. Then, preheat the oven to 400°F.

2. Peel and crush the garlic and put it into a saucepan with the olive oil. Then, add the chopped tomatoes, sugar, herbs and a pinch each of salt and of pepper.

4. When the dough has been in a warm place for 1½ hours, lift it out and put it on a floury surface. Knead it for about a minute, to squeeze out any air bubbles.

6. Using a paper towel, wipe a little oil over a large baking sheet. Then, sprinkle more flour on the floury surface and on a rolling pin. Put the dough on the surface.

Spread out the sauce with
the back of a spoon.

7. Roll out the dough until it is
about 12 inches across, then lift
it onto the baking sheet. Spread
the tomato sauce on it, leaving
a border around the edge.

8. Sprinkle about two-thirds of the
cheese over the tomato sauce.
Arrange the pepperoni and olives
on the cheese, then sprinkle the
rest of the cheese over them.

9. Bake the pizza in the oven for
about 20 minutes, until the crust
is crisp and the cheese is golden
brown and bubbling. Then, cut
it into slices with a sharp knife.

# Salmon fishcakes

These crispy oven-baked fishcakes are filling and easy to make. Instead of making them with salmon, you could use haddock or smoked haddock instead.

Try serving the fishcakes with French-cut green beans. Trim off the ends of the beans and cook them in boiling water for about 10 minutes, or until they are just tender.

## Ingredients:

Serves 4

12 oz. fresh salmon fillets
1 bay leaf
a small handful of fresh parsley
1 lb. potatoes
1 tablespoon butter
salt and ground black pepper
1 medium egg
about 3 tablespoons all-purpose
    flour
2 oz. (3 slices) white bread, with
    the crusts removed
1 tablespoon sunflower oil

Keep the parsley leaves for later.

1. Put the salmon into a large pan, in a single layer. Pour in enough water to just cover it. Add the bay leaf, then break the stalks off the parsley and add them too.

The salmon turns pale pink as it cooks.

2. Heat the pan until the water boils, then reduce the heat, so that the water is just bubbling. Cook the salmon for four minutes, then take the pan off the heat.

3. Using a spatula, lift out the salmon and put it onto a plate to cool. Clean the pan thoroughly, then half-fill it with cold water and add two pinches of salt.

4. Peel the potatoes and cut them into large chunks. Put them into the pan, then heat the water until it boils. Reduce the heat a little, so that the water is gently bubbling.

Squeeze fresh lemon juice over the fishcakes.

5. Cook the potatoes for 15-20 minutes, or until they are tender. While they are cooking, break the salmon into flakes, with a fork. Remove the skin and any bones.

## Chef's Tip

Flaking fish is a good idea, because you should be able to see any little bones. Fillets of fish shouldn't have any bones in them, but it's a good idea to check.

Keep mashing until the potato is smooth.

6. Drain the potatoes through a colander, then pour them back into the pan. Add the butter, a pinch of salt and a pinch of black pepper, then mash the potatoes.

7. Put the parsley leaves into a mug and chop them with kitchen scissors. Then, break the egg into a bowl and beat the white and yolk with a fork.

8. Add the salmon, parsley leaves and a tablespoon of beaten egg to the potatoes and stir everything together. Then, preheat your oven to 400°F.

The flour keeps the mixture from sticking to your hands.

9. Divide the salmon mixture into eight pieces. Then, put a little flour on your hands. Shape each piece into a slightly flattened round, about ¾ inch thick.

10. Using a food processor, make the bread into fine breadcrumbs (see page 94) and put them into a bowl. Then, using a paper towel, wipe the oil over a baking tray.

The breadcrumbs stick to the egg.

11. Brush egg all over a fishcake, then roll the fishcake in the breadcrumbs, until it is completely covered. Then, prepare the other fishcakes in the same way.

Wear oven mitts to take the baking tray out of the oven.

12. Put the fishcakes on the baking tray and put them in the oven for 10 minutes. Lift them out and turn them, then cook them for 10 more minutes, until they are crispy.

# Rice

Rice is often eaten with meat, fish or vegetables. Here, you can find out how to cook it and some information about different kinds of rice, too.

## Ways to cook

Rice can be boiled or steamed. The most common cooking method is using just enough water, as shown below. Some rice needs to be soaked before it's cooked, so always check the instructions on the package. Also look to see how much rice you need for each person. If it doesn't say on the package, 1/3 cup will be about right for each person, to accompany a main meal.

## Boiling in lots of water

1. Half-fill a pan with water and add a pinch of salt. Heat the water until it boils, add the rice and bring it back to a boil.

2. Turn down the heat a little and cook the rice for as long as it says on the package. Then, drain it through a large sieve.

White rice has had its outer coating removed.

'Instant' and 'Quick-cook' rice are treated so that the grains don't stick together when the rice is cooked.

Mixed rice contains two or more different kinds of rice. The rice grains are treated so that they will cook in the same amount of time.

## Just enough water

Brown rice needs an extra half cup of water per person.

1. To cook rice without having to drain it, put one cup of rice and two cups of water for each person in a pan.

The water should be bubbling gently.

2. Add a pinch of salt and heat the water until it boils. Stir the rice, then reduce the heat a little. Put a lid on the pan.

Don't lift the lid while the rice is cooking.

3. Cook the rice for as long as it says on the package. If any water is left, heat the pan for another minute.

## Chef's Tip

When you cook rice, if the water turns thick and sticky, tip the rice into a sieve and rinse it with boiling water.

Brown rice still has its outer coating and is chewier than white rice. It needs to be cooked for longer than white rice.

Arborio rice is sticky and is used to make risotto (see pages 36-37).

Wild rice is not actually rice at all. It's a type of seed from the USA and Canada. It should be soaked for at least an hour, then cooked for about 40 minutes.

Thai or Jasmine rice is very sticky, which makes it easier to eat with chopsticks. Here you can see it cooked and uncooked.

Basmati rice needs to be soaked before it's cooked. Try eating it with creamy chicken (pages 42-43).

## Steamed rice

Steaming works better with white rice than brown rice.

1. Soak the rice in cold water for one hour, then drain it through a sieve. Half-fill a pan with water and heat it until it boils.

2. Put the rice into a steamer. Put the steamer on top of the pan. Cook the rice for at least 20 minutes, until it is tender.

Short-grain rice is used to make rice pudding, which is a sweet dish.

Red Carmargue rice has a nutty taste. It needs to be washed then boiled for about 30 minutes.

33

# Chili con carne

The name of this dish means 'chili with meat'. It can be served with rice, but is usually served over corn chips, with pasta, or spooned into a baked potato (see page 65).

## Ingredients:

Serves 4

half a beef or vegetable bouillon cube
1 onion
1 clove of garlic
1½ tablespoons vegetable oil
1 lb. extra-lean ground beef
2-4 teaspoons mild chili powder
1 teaspoon ground cumin
14 oz. can red kidney beans
14 oz. can chopped tomatoes
6 oz. can tomato paste
1 teaspoon brown sugar
½ teaspoon mixed seasoning
salt and ground black pepper

1. Put the bouillon cube into a heatproof container and pour in 1 cup of boiling water. Stir the broth until the cube has dissolved, then put the container to the side.

2. Peel the onion and cut it in half. Cut it into slices, then cut the slices into small pieces. Peel and crush the garlic. Put the pieces of onion, garlic and oil into a large saucepan.

## Chef's Tip

3. Gently heat the pan on low heat for 10 minutes, stirring the onion and garlic frequently. Then, increase the heat to medium and add the ground beef.

4. Cook the beef for about 10 minutes, or until it is brown all over. Break up any lumps with a wooden spoon and keep stirring it as it cooks.

You're about to add chili powder to the beef. If you pour spices from the jar into a spoon over a pan, you may add too much, so do it away from the pan instead.

5. Take the pan off the heat and stir in the chili powder and cumin. Then, open the can of kidney beans. Pour them into a colander and rinse them under cold water.

6. Add the beans, tomatoes, broth, tomato paste, sugar and seasoning to the pan. Add two pinches of salt and of pepper, then stir everything together.

The steam escapes through the gap.

7. Put the pan back on the heat and heat it until the chili con carne boils. Stir the chili, then reduce the heat to low. Put a lid on the pan, leaving a small gap.

8. Cook the chili for 15 minutes, then remove the lid and cook it for another 15 minutes. Make sure you stir the chili every now and then, to keep it from sticking.

35

# Vegetable risotto

Risotto is made with arborio rice, which becomes sticky when it's cooked. In this recipe, the rice is cooked in broth and vegetables are added as it cooks. If you're really hungry, serve the risotto with bread rolls.

## Ingredients:

Serves 4

4 ripe tomatoes
½ cup frozen peas
½ cup chopped (or 1 stalk)
  broccoli
2 oz. (½ cup) Parmesan cheese
1 onion
1 clove of garlic
1 tablespoon butter
1 tablespoon of olive oil
1 cup arborio (risotto) rice
1 vegetable bouillon cube
2 tablespoons chopped fresh
  parsley
salt and ground black pepper

1. Cut a cross on the bottom of each tomato with a sharp knife. Put the tomatoes in a heatproof bowl, then fill another bowl with cold water.

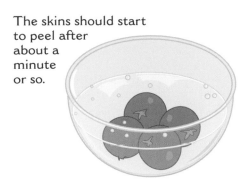

The skins should start to peel after about a minute or so.

2. Pour boiling water over the tomatoes. When their skins start to peel, lift them out with a slotted spoon and put them into the cold water for two minutes.

Throw away the skins, cores and seeds.

3. Lift the tomatoes out and peel off the skins. Cut each tomato into quarters, then scoop out the seeds and cut out the cores. Then, cut the quarters into small pieces.

4. Put the peas onto a plate to defrost. Cut the end off the stem of the broccoli and throw it away. Cut off the curly parts, cut them into pieces, then slice the stem.

5. Grate the Parmesan on the fine holes on a grater. Then, peel an onion and cut it in half. Finely slice it, then cut the slices into small pieces. Peel the clove of garlic.

Keep stirring the onion and garlic.

6. Put the butter, oil and onion into a large saucepan. Crush the garlic into the pan, then heat the pan over a medium heat for five minutes, or until the onion is soft.

7. Take the pan off the heat. Add the rice to the pan and stir it in, to coat the grains of rice with the butter mixture. Then, put the bouillon cube into another pan.

8. Add 3½ cups of boiling water and stir it well. Gently heat the broth, until it starts to bubble, then add a ladleful to the rice and put the rice back on the heat.

Use a wooden spoon.

You may not need to use all the broth.

9. Gently stir the rice until almost all of the liquid has been absorbed. Then, add the broccoli and another ladleful of broth. Each time the broth is absorbed, stir in more.

10. About 15 minutes after you added the first broth, stir in the peas. Keep adding ladlefuls of broth and stirring them in, until the rice is creamy and tender.

11. Take the pan off the heat and cover it with a lid. Leave it for three minutes, then stir in the tomatoes, parsley, Parmesan and two pinches of salt and of pepper.

# Chicken stir-fry

Stir-fries are quick and easy to cook. In this recipe, the chicken is soaked in a marinade, which is a sauce that helps to make meat tender and tasty.

## Ingredients:

Serves 4

1 inch piece of fresh root ginger
1 tablespoon honey
3 tablespoons soy sauce
1 tablespoon fresh lemon juice
3 skinless, boneless chicken
   breasts
2 carrots
1 yellow or red pepper
8 green onions
½ cup (4 oz.) sugar snap or
   snow peas
2 tablespoons sunflower oil
½ teaspoon cornstarch
a vegetable bouillon cube

## Chef's Tip

When you cook a stir-fry, you add lots of different ingredients and cook them quickly, so you prepare all the ingredients before you start cooking.

1. Cut the brown skin off the ginger and throw it away. Cut the ginger into thin slices and cut the slices into thin sticks. Then, cut the sticks into tiny pieces.

2. For the marinade, put the ginger in a bowl. Add the honey, soy sauce and lemon juice. Then, cut any pieces of white fat off the chicken breasts and throw them away.

3. Cut the chicken into strips. Stir the strips into the marinade, then wash your hands (see the Chef's tip on page 42). Then, peel the carrots with a potato peeler.

**You don't need the ends or the seeds.**

4. Cut the ends off the pepper, remove the seeds and cut it into strips. Then, cut the ends off the carrots. Cut them in half, then in half again, then into thin sticks.

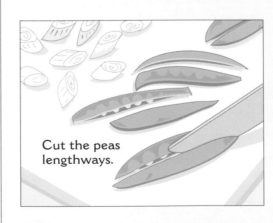

Cut the peas lengthways.

5. Cut the ends and outer layer off the green onions. Cut the ends off the peas. Then, cut the onions into diagonal slices and cut the peas in half.

6. Put the bouillon cube into a heatproof container. Pour in 1 cup of boiling water and stir it until the cube dissolves. Then, put the container off to the side.

Use a spoon to
add the chicken.

The stir-fry can be
served with egg
noodles or rice.

7. Heat one tablespoon of oil in
a large frying pan, for one minute,
on medium heat. Carefully add the
chicken to the pan, but don't add
the marinade yet.

8. Cook the chicken for five
minutes, stirring it all the time.
Then, take it out of the pan with
a slotted spoon and put it on a
plate. Put the chicken aside.

Stir the vegetables
all the time.

Stir the broth
with a fork, as
you add the
marinade.

9. Add the other tablespoon of oil
to the pan and heat it for about 20
seconds. Then, add the pieces of
carrot and peas and cook them for
two minutes.

10. Add the green onions and
strips of pepper and cook them
for one minute. Mix the cornstarch
into the marinade, then mix the
marinade into the broth.

11. Pour the broth into the pan and
stir everything well. Then, stir in
the chicken. Heat the stir-fry until
the broth boils, then gently cook
everything for three minutes.

39

# Herbs and spices

Herbs and spices are used to flavor food. They are cooked with meat, fish and vegetables, but can also be used to add flavor to sauces, salads and even sweet things.

Bay leaves are used to flavor stews and soups, like the potato soup on pages 10-11. They are removed before the food is served.

## Herbs

You can use fresh or dried herbs when you cook. If a recipe uses fresh herbs but you only have dried ones, use half the amount, as dried herbs taste a lot stronger.

Parsley is used in lots of recipes. It is also used to decorate food.

## Preparing fresh herbs

Dill is eaten with fish and can also be mixed into salads.

1. Wash the herbs and dry them on some paper towels. Then, cut off any thick or woody stalks and throw them away.

Basil tastes delicious with tomatoes (see pages 48-49) and can be ripped up and scattered on salads.

Dried mixed herbs are a mixture of several different herbs and are included in all kinds of dishes.

2. Put the soft parts of the herbs into a cup. To finely chop them, snip them with kitchen scissors again and again.

Fresh coriander has a very strong flavor. It is used in the tomato salsa on pages 22-23.

## Chives

Mint has a fresh taste. It is often used to decorate food.

You don't need to trim chives before you chop them. Just hold several chives together and snip them into tiny pieces.

Chives have a mild onion flavor.

Oregano is used fresh or dried.

# Spices

Spices come from different parts of plants, such as berries, roots, bark and seeds. They are not always hot, but many have strong and distinctive flavors.

Most of the spices used in this book are in a crushed or powdered form. Whole spices can also be crushed, using a pestle and mortar.

Coriander seeds have a delicious, light flavor when they're crushed.

Cumin seeds are used a lot in Indian cooking.

Ground coriander tastes slightly sweet.

Cinnamon sticks

Cinnamon is the bark of a tree. The sticks are used in spicy dishes and are not eaten. Ground cinnamon is used to flavor sweet dishes, such as apple crumble (see pages 80-81).

This is ground cumin. It is strong, with a warm flavor.

Turmeric has a strong, slightly bitter flavor.

Paprika is spicy and is made from the seeds of sweet peppers.

Ginger can be used fresh, as a root (see pages 38-39), or dried and ground.

Dried chilies

Ground ginger

Chilies are very hot and spicy. They can be bought fresh, dried or as a powder.

Chili powder

Whole nutmeg seeds are grated to make a fine powder.

# Creamy chicken

This delicious chicken dish has a mild, creamy flavor. It is made with yogurt, coconut milk and a hint of spices. Serve it with boiled or steamed rice (see pages 32-33).

## Ingredients:

Serves 4

4 skinless, boneless chicken
   breasts
2 level teaspoons cornstarch
1 cup (8 oz.) thick plain yogurt
1 chicken bouillon cube
1 onion
2 tablespoons vegetable oil
2 cloves of garlic
½ teaspoon ground turmeric
½ teaspoon ground ginger
1 teaspoon ground cumin
2 teaspoons ground coriander
½ cup coconut milk
salt and ground black pepper
2 tablespoons chopped fresh
   coriander

## Chef's Tip

Whenever you cook chicken, you need to wash your hands before handling any other food. Make sure you use a separate cutting board or plate, too.

Throw away any pieces of fat.

1. Using a sharp knife, cut any pieces of white fat off the chicken breasts. Cut each chicken breast into three equal-sized pieces, then wash your hands thoroughly.

3. Put the bouillon cube into a heatproof container and pour in ⅓ cup of boiling water. Then, stir the water until the cube dissolves completely.

5. Take the pan off the heat. Then, peel and crush the garlic. Add the crushed garlic to the pan, then add the ground turmeric, ginger, cumin and coriander, too.

2. Put the cornstarch into a bowl. Add two tablespoons of yogurt and mix them in well. Then, mix in the rest of the yogurt, a little at a time.

Stir the onion as it cooks.

4. Cut the ends off the onion and peel it. Cut it in half, then into small pieces. Put the pieces into a large saucepan with the oil. Cook them on low heat for 10 minutes.

6. Gently heat the pan for two minutes and keep stirring it. Turn the heat down very low and add the chicken. Stir in the yogurt mixture, one tablespoon at a time.

This creamy chicken is served with Basmati rice and decorated with a sprig of fresh coriander.

If you're serving rice with the creamy chicken, you'll need to start cooking it while the chicken is cooking in step 8.

The steam escapes through the gap.

Uncooked chicken will still be pink.

7. Stir the coconut milk and broth into the mixture, a little at a time. Mix in a pinch of salt and of pepper, then put a lid on the pan, leaving a small gap on one side.

8. Cook the mixture on low heat for 30 minutes, stirring it every now and then. Then, take out a piece of chicken and cut it in half. If it is white inside, it is cooked.

9. If the chicken is slightly pink inside, cook it for another 5-10 minutes. Then, stir in the fresh coriander and serve the creamy chicken immediately.

# Spaghetti bolognese

This tasty meat sauce is usually served with spaghetti, but it can also be layered with a white sauce and sheets of pasta, to make lasagna (see pages 60-61).

## Ingredients:

Serves 4

1 onion
1 carrot
1 stick of celery
2 tablespoons olive oil
1 clove of garlic
1 lb. extra-lean ground beef
1 beef or vegetable bouillon
   cube
14 oz. can chopped tomatoes
1 teaspoon Italian seasoning
6 oz. can tomato paste
salt and ground black pepper
½ tablespoon olive oil
14 oz. dried spaghetti

## Chef's Tip

To see if pasta is cooked, lift out a piece with a spoon, rinse it under cold water and bite it. It should be tender but not soggy. This is known as 'al dente' in Italy.

You don't need the ends of the celery.

1. Peel the onion and cut it in half. Slice it and chop it finely. Then, peel the carrot and cut off its ends. Cut it in half, then cut it into strips. Cut the strips into small pieces.

2. Wash the celery, and cut off its ends. Cut it into small pieces. Put the onion and the olive oil into a large saucepan. Cook them on medium heat for five minutes.

3. Peel the garlic and crush it into the pan, then add the pieces of carrot and celery. Heat everything for two minutes, stirring them all the time with a wooden spoon.

4. Add the beef to the pan and cook it for about 10 minutes, or until it is brown all over. Break up any lumps with the spoon and keep stirring it as it cooks.

5. Put the bouillon cube into a heatproof container. Add 1 cup of boiling water, and stir it until the bouillon cube has dissolved. Then, add the broth to the pan.

6. Add the chopped tomatoes, seasoning, tomato paste and a couple of pinches of salt and of pepper to the pan. Heat the sauce until it boils, then reduce the heat.

The sauce should be gently bubbling.

Push in the ends of the spaghetti with a wooden spoon.

7. Put the lid on the pan, leaving a small gap. Cook the sauce for 40 minutes, stirring it every now and then. Then, remove the lid and cook it for 10 more minutes.

8. While the sauce is cooking, fill a large pan with water and add a large pinch of salt. Add half a tablespoon of olive oil, then heat the pan until the water boils.

9. Lower one end of the spaghetti into the water. As it softens, bend it around until it is covered by the water. Boil it for as long as it says on the package, stirring often.

10. Carefully pour the spaghetti into a colander in the sink and gently shake the colander. Then, put some spaghetti on each plate, and spoon some sauce over it.

Serve the spaghetti bolognese with some grated Parmesan cheese sprinkled over the top.

# Fettuccine carbonara

This egg-based pasta dish is quick and simple to make. The eggs are cooked by the heat of the pasta and make a creamy sauce. Fettuccine pasta is used here, but you can use any long thin pasta, such as spaghetti or linguine.

## Ingredients:

Serves 4

1 teaspoon olive oil
5 oz. (7-8 slices) bacon
2 cloves of garlic
2 oz. (½ cup) Parmesan
  cheese
3 medium eggs
2 tablespoons fresh parsley,
  chopped
3 tablespoons light cream
ground black pepper
12 oz. dried fettuccine

Don't crush the garlic cloves.

1. Half-fill a large saucepan with water and add a teaspoon of olive oil. Heat the water until it boils, then switch off the heat and put the pan to the side.

2. Using clean kitchen scissors, cut across the slices of bacon to make pieces like the ones shown here. Then, put the pieces into a saucepan.

3. Peel the cloves of garlic, but don't crush them. Add them to the pan. Heat the pan on medium heat for 3-4 minutes, until the bacon is crispy.

The paper towel absorbs the oil on the bacon.

4. Turn off the heat. Lift the bacon out of the pan with a spoon and put it on some paper towels. Throw away the garlic cloves, which will have added flavor.

5. Grate the cheese on the fine holes on a grater. Then, break the eggs into a bowl and add half of the cheese, the chopped parsley, the cream and a pinch of black pepper.

6. Mix everything in the bowl with a fork. Then, heat the pan of water until it is boiling again. Add the pasta and cook it for as long as it says on the package.

## Chef's Tip

When you're boiling pasta, keep an eye on it, in case it boils too hard. If it looks as if it's about to boil over, turn down the heat a little, but keep the water bubbling.

7. When the pasta is cooked, turn off the heat, then pour it into a colander in the sink. Shake the colander, then pour the pasta back into the pan and add the bacon.

8. Pour in the egg mixture and cook on low heat, until there is no liquid egg left. Then, spoon the pasta into four bowls and sprinkle the rest of the cheese over it.

# Pasta with fresh tomato sauce

This pasta dish tastes really fresh and is ideal as a light meal. To make it taste really good, use the ripest tomatoes and the freshest basil you can find.

## Ingredients:

Serves 4

For the sauce:
1½ lbs. ripe tomatoes
2 cloves of garlic
1 tablespoon olive oil
½ teaspoon dried oregano
   or Italian seasoning
a pinch of sugar
salt and ground black pepper
about 12 fresh basil leaves

For the pasta:
1 tablespoon olive oil
salt
12 oz. dried pasta shapes

If you want to serve the pasta at the table, put all the pasta into a big bowl, like this, and spoon the sauce on top.

1. Cut a cross on the bottom of each tomato with a sharp knife. Put the tomatoes into a heatproof bowl, then fill a second bowl with cold water.

2. Pour boiling water over the tomatoes, until they are completely covered. Leave them in the water for about a minute, until their skins start to peel off.

Make sure your hands are clean.

3. Lift the tomatoes out with a slotted spoon, then put them into the cold water for two minutes. Lift them out, peel off their skins, then cut each one into quarters.

4. Scoop out the seeds with a teaspoon. Carefully cut out the green core and cut all the quarters into small pieces. Then, peel the garlic and crush it.

The steam escapes through the gap.

5. Put the garlic, a tablespoon of olive oil, the tomatoes, seasoning, sugar and a pinch of salt and of pepper into a pan. Heat the pan on medium heat for two minutes.

6. Cover the pan with a lid, leaving a small gap, and turn down the heat. Cook the sauce on low heat for 10-15 minutes, stirring it often, to keep it from sticking.

7. Meanwhile, half-fill a large pan with water. Add a tablespoon of olive oil and a pinch of salt. Heat the water until it boils, then add the pasta to the pan and stir it.

8. Heat the pan until the water is boiling again. Then, turn down the heat, so that the water is bubbling more gently. Cook the pasta for as long as it says on the package.

9. While the pasta is cooking, stir the tomato sauce every now and then. Pour the cooked pasta into a colander and drain it well, by gently shaking the colander.

10. Rip the basil leaves into small pieces and stir them into the tomato sauce. Then, spoon the sauce over the top of the pasta, to serve it.

This kind of pasta is farfalle, but you can use any shape.

# Macaroni and cheese

This macaroni and cheese has a crunchy topping. It's quick to cook and goes really well with a sliced tomato salad.

## Ingredients:

Serves 4

salt
8 oz. dried macaroni
1 cup (8 oz.) Cheddar cheese
small amount of butter
4 tablespoons butter or margarine
½ cup all-purpose flour
2¼ cups milk
½ teaspoon mustard
salt and ground black pepper
2 slices of bread, crusts removed

For the tomato salad:
8 ripe tomatoes
½ tablespoon chopped chives

1. Half-fill a saucepan with water and add two pinches of salt. Heat the water until it boils, then add the macaroni. Cook the macaroni for as long as it says on the package.

2. Meanwhile, grate the cheese on the medium holes on a grater. When the macaroni is cooked, pour it into a colander and drain it well, by gently shaking the colander.

**Don't put the pan back on the heat.**

**Add the flour slowly, to avoid making lumps.**

3. Spoon the macaroni back into the pan and stir in a little butter, to stop the pieces from sticking together. Then, cover the pan with a lid, to keep the macaroni warm.

4. Put 4 tablespoons of butter into a large pan, and heat it on low heat until it melts. Take the pan off the heat, then stir in the flour, a little at a time.

Use a wooden spoon.

It's really important to keep stirring the sauce.

## Chef's Tip

5. Add a little milk to the pan. Stir it in really well, until the mixture is smooth. Then, stir in a little more milk. Continue until you have added all the milk.

6. Heat the sauce on medium heat, stirring all the time, until it becomes thicker and then boils. Boil it for one minute, still stirring it, then take it off the heat.

If your sauce is a little lumpy when you take it off the heat, it's easy to make it smooth. Twist a whisk around and around in the pan, until the lumps have gone.

Keep some of the cheese for the topping.

7. Stir the mustard, macaroni and a pinch of salt and of pepper into the sauce. Heat the pan for about 30 seconds. Take it off the heat. Then, stir in three-quarters of the cheese.

8. Pour a little cooking oil into an ovenproof dish. Wipe the oil over the inside of the dish with a paper towel, then turn on your oven's broiler for five minutes.

9. While the broiler is heating up, make the breadcrumbs for the topping. Put the bread into a food processor (see page 94) and make it into breadcrumbs.

Lay the halves flat side down.

10. Spoon the macaroni into the dish and sprinkle the breadcrumbs over the top. Then, sprinkle the rest of the grated cheese over the breadcrumbs.

11. Carefully put the dish in the broiler and leave the macaroni to cook for 3-4 minutes, until it turns golden. Then, carefully remove the dish, wearing oven mitts.

12. For the salad, cut the tomatoes in half, cut out the core and throw it away. Cut the tomatoes into slices, then put them into a bowl. Sprinkle chopped chives over the top.

# Vegetables

Lots of the recipes in this book include vegetables, cooked in a variety of ways. On these pages, you'll find out more about preparing different kinds of vegetables.

## A good rinse

Unless told otherwise, always rinse vegetables and salad ingredients. Gently rinse delicate vegetables such as mushrooms, then dry them with paper towels.

## Hot or cold water?

Some vegetables are put in boiling water to be cooked, and others are placed in a pan of cold water and brought to a boil. In general, root vegetables (such as potatoes, carrots and turnips) are cooked from cold, and the others are placed in water which has already boiled. To find out more about how to cook potatoes, see pages 64-65.

Find out how to prepare tomatoes in step 2 on page 4.

# Chopping an onion

Throw the skin and ends away.

1. Using a sharp knife, carefully cut off both ends of the onion. Then, cut down one side and peel off the skin.

2. With a flat side facing down, cut the onion in half. Cut each half into slices, then chop the slices into small pieces.

# Peeling garlic

Throw the ends and skin away.

1. To remove a clove from a head of garlic, press against the side of the stem. When the skin splits, break it open.

2. To peel the clove, cut off its ends, then make a cut down the skin. Then, peel off the skin with your fingers.

# Preparing peppers

1. Using a sharp knife, carefully cut off the ends of the pepper. Then, cut the pepper in half, from top to bottom.

2. Remove the lines of white seeds with your fingers. Throw away the ends of the pepper and the seeds.

# Broccoli

Floret

Throw this piece away.

1. Put the broccoli on a cutting board, and cut off the tough end of the main stem. Then, cut off the individual florets.

2. Put the florets into a colander. Rinse them thoroughly under cold running water, then shake them dry.

# Mushrooms

Throw this piece away.

Rinse each mushroom under running water and blot them dry with a paper towel. Then, cut off the end of the stem.

# Cleaning leeks

Throw the ends away.

1. If a leek is dirty, cut off the tough green top and trim off the root. Then, cut all the way down, from end to end.

2. To remove any mud or dirt inside, rinse each half of the leek really well under running water, until it is clean.

3. Shake the pieces of leek to remove the water. Then, lay them on a cutting board and slice across them.

# Ratatouille with butter bean mash

**R**atatouille is a mixture of fresh vegetables in a tomato sauce. Here it is served with butter bean mash, making a complete vegetarian meal.

## Ingredients:

Serves 4

2 onions
1 lb. (about 4 medium) ripe
   tomatoes
3 zucchini
1 eggplant, weighing about 1 lb.
1 yellow or red pepper
3 tablespoons olive oil
1 clove of garlic
½ can (3 oz.) tomato paste
½ teaspoon dried oregano
   or Italian seasoning
salt and ground black pepper
8 large basil leaves

For the butter bean mash:
two 14 oz. cans of butter beans
1 tablespoon butter
salt and ground black pepper
2 tablespoons chopped fresh
   parsley

Throw away the cores.

1. Peel the onions and cut them in half. Cut them into slices, then cut the slices into small pieces. Then, peel the tomatoes, cut them into quarters and cut out the cores.

2. Cut the ends off the zucchini and throw them away. Cut each zucchini in half lengthways, then cut the halves in half, to make strips. Cut the strips into chunks.

Ratatouille is also delicious served with grilled meat or fish.

3. Prepare the eggplant in the same way as the zucchini. Then, cut the ends off the yellow pepper and remove the seeds. Cut the pepper into thin strips, lengthways.

4. Put the oil and the onions into a large saucepan. Cook the onions over a low heat for about 10 minutes, until they are soft and starting to turn golden.

5. Peel and crush the garlic and add it to the pan. Then, add all of the prepared vegetables, tomato paste, herbs and a pinch of salt and of pepper. Stir everything well.

Watch out for the hot steam when you lift the lid.

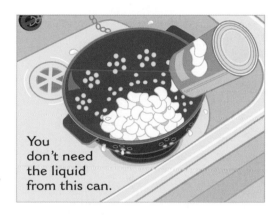

You don't need the liquid from this can.

6. Cook the ratatouille on medium heat for about three minutes, stirring it often. Then, turn down the heat, so that it is bubbling gently.

7. Cover the pan with its lid and cook the ratatouille for 20 minutes, stirring it every now and then. Then, remove the lid and cook it for another 10 minutes.

8. Meanwhile, open both cans of butter beans. Pour the contents of one can, including the liquid, into a saucepan. Pour the contents of the other can into a colander.

If the mash is a little dry, mix in a few drops of milk.

9. Rinse the beans in the colander with cold water, then drain them. Pour the rinsed beans into the saucepan, then add the butter and a pinch of salt and of pepper.

10. Heat the pan until the liquid is gently boiling, then turn the heat down low. Cook the beans for five minutes, until they are very soft. Then, turn off the heat.

11. Mash the beans well, then stir in the chopped parsley. Tear the basil leaves into small pieces and stir them into the ratatouille, before serving it with the mash.

# Vegetable crumble

This savory crumble is topped with a delicious mixture of oats, nuts and cheese. The vegetable filling includes sweet potatoes, which have a rich, sweet flavor.

## Ingredients:

Serves 4

For the crumble topping:
1 cup all-purpose flour
¼ cup butter
2 oz. (½ cup) Cheddar cheese
¼ cup chopped mixed nuts
2 tablespoons rolled oats

For the vegetable filling:
2 leeks
4 oz. (about 3 medium)
    mushrooms
1 carrot
1 lb. sweet potatoes
a vegetable bouillon cube
2 tablespoons butter
1 tablespoon all-purpose flour
2 oz. cream cheese
salt and ground black pepper

1. For the topping, sift the flour through a sieve into a large bowl. Cut the butter into cubes and add them to the flour. Rub the butter into the flour with your fingers.

2. Grate the Cheddar cheese on the big holes on a grater. Add it to the bowl, then add the nuts and oats. Stir all the ingredients until they are mixed together well.

3. Preheat the oven to 375°F. While it is heating up, cut the ends off the leeks. Wash the leeks thoroughly in cold water, then cut them into thin slices.

4. Rinse the mushrooms and blot off any excess water. Cut off the ends. Then, peel the carrot with a potato peeler. Cut off the ends, then cut it into about six chunks.

Keep the heat low.

5. Peel the sweet potatoes. Cut each potato in half, then into ¾ inch cubes. Then, put the bouillon cube into a heatproof container and add ½ cup of boiling water.

6. Stir the water until the cube has completely dissolved. Then, put the butter into a large pan and gently heat the pan on low heat, until the butter melts.

7. Put the leeks into the pan and put on the lid, leaving a gap. Cook the leeks for three minutes. Gently shake the pan every now and then, to keep them from sticking.

## Chef's Tip

8. Remove the lid, then add the mushrooms, carrots and sweet potatoes to the pan. Cook them gently for five minutes, stirring them often.

In the next step, you're going to add the flour and broth to the pan. To keep the flour from going lumpy, add a little broth at a time, mix it in, then add some more.

9. Sprinkle the flour over the vegetables and stir it in well. Pour in the broth. Then, stir in the cream cheese and add two pinches of salt and of pepper.

10. Heat the vegetable mixture on medium heat for two minutes, so that it is bubbling gently. Then, spoon the mixture into an ovenproof dish.

11. Spoon the topping over the vegetables. Then, put the dish on a baking tray. Bake the crumble in the oven for 30-35 minutes or until the topping is golden brown.

# Lamb kebabs

As in the stir-fry on pages 38-39, the meat in this recipe is soaked in a marinade. The kebabs are delicious in a pitta bread with shredded lettuce, cucumber, mint and lemon juice.

## Ingredients:

Serves 4

For the marinade:
1 tablespoon of fresh lemon juice
4 tablespoons olive oil
a large pinch of dried oregano
salt and ground black pepper
1 clove of garlic

For the kebabs:
2 large lamb steaks, each
    about 6 oz.
1 red onion
1 red pepper
2 zucchini

8 kebab or satay sticks

## Chef's Tip

To avoid burning the kebabs, don't put them too close to the heat. When they are on the rack, they should be about 3 inches below the heat.

1. For the marinade, put the lemon juice into a bowl with the oil, dried oregano and a pinch of salt and of pepper. Peel the garlic, crush it into the bowl and stir everything well.

2. If you're using wooden sticks, put them into a dish of water to soak. This helps to keep them from burning when you cook the kebabs.

**Throw away the bone and fat.**

3. Using a sharp knife, carefully cut out any bone and trim the fat off the lamb. Then, cut the lamb into ¾ inch cubes. Add them to the marinade and stir them in well.

4. Cover the bowl with plastic foodwrap. Put it in the refrigerator for at least an hour, so that the meat soaks in the marinade. While it is soaking, prepare the vegetables.

**Throw away the ends and the seeds.**

5. Cut the ends off the onion and peel it. Cut the onion in half, then in half again. Then, cut across each quarter. Separate each chunk into double slices, like this.

6. Cut the ends off the red pepper. Remove the seeds. Cut the pepper into ¾ inch squares. Then, cut off the ends of the zucchini and cut them into thick slices.

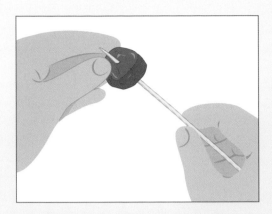

7. Take the wooden sticks out of the water. Then, carefully push one cube of lamb onto each wooden stick, being careful of the pointed end.

Mix up the pieces of meat and vegetables.

8. Push pieces of vegetables and lamb onto the wooden sticks, until you have used up all of the pieces. Then, turn on your oven's broiler or start up your grill.

Lay the kebabs on the rack in a grill pan.

9. Brush the vegetables with the marinade, so that they don't dry out while they're cooking. Then, put the kebabs on the grill or in your oven's broiler for 10 minutes.

10. After 10 minutes, carefully turn the kebabs over. Spoon the rest of the marinade over them, then grill them for another 5-10 minutes, or until they are browned.

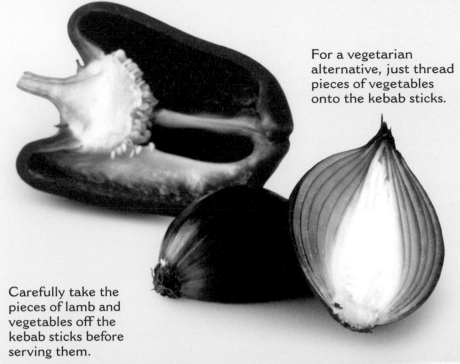

For a vegetarian alternative, just thread pieces of vegetables onto the kebab sticks.

Carefully take the pieces of lamb and vegetables off the kebab sticks before serving them.

Squeeze fresh lemon juice over the cooked lamb.

# Lasagna

Lasagna is made up of layers of white sauce, bolognese sauce and pasta. For a vegetarian alternative, use ratatouille (see pages 54-55) instead of bolognese sauce.

## Ingredients:

Serves 4

For the bolognese sauce:
1 onion
1 carrot
1 stick of celery
2 tablespoons olive oil
1 clove of garlic
1 lb. extra-lean ground beef
1 beef or vegetable bouillon
   cube
14 oz. can chopped tomatoes
6 oz. can tomato paste
1 teaspoon Italian seasoning
salt and ground black pepper

For the white sauce:
1 tablespoon butter
2 tablespoons all-purpose flour
1 cup milk
a pinch of grated nutmeg
salt and ground black pepper

6 oz. (6 noodles) dried lasagne
1 oz. (1/8 cup) Parmesan cheese

Remember to keep stirring the bolognese sauce.

1. To make the bolognese sauce, follow steps 1-7 on pages 44-45. When you get to step 7, and the bolognese sauce is gently bubbling, start to make the white sauce.

2. To make the white sauce, follow steps 4-6 on pages 50-51, using the amounts in this recipe. Take the pan off the heat, then stir in a pinch of salt, of pepper and of nutmeg.

3. Preheat the oven to 350°F. While it is heating up, wipe a paper towel in some butter, then wipe butter over the inside of an ovenproof dish.

4. Spoon half of the bolognese sauce into the dish and spread it out with the back of the spoon. Then, place a single layer of lasagne on top of the sauce.

# Chef's Tip

If the sheets of lasagne don't fit the shape of your dish, break some of them into smaller pieces. Lay down the big pieces first, then fill in the gaps with small pieces.

Make sure that the white sauce goes to the edges of the dish.

5. Spoon the rest of the bolognese sauce over the lasagne, then add another layer of lasagne. Then, spoon the white sauce over the top, so that the lasagne is covered.

6. Grate the Parmesan cheese on the fine holes on a grater, then sprinkle it over the top. Then, put the dish on a baking sheet, in case any sauce bubbles over.

7. Bake the lasagna in the oven for 35-45 minutes, or until the top is browned and bubbling. Then, carefully lift it out, wearing oven mitts. It will be very hot.

8. Push a sharp knife into the middle of the lasagna. If it is cooked, the knife will slide in easily. If it's not cooked, cook it for another 5-10 minutes.

Let the lasagna cool for five minutes, then serve it with a crunchy green salad (see pages 8-9).

# Oven-roasted vegetables

This recipe is a really easy way to cook potatoes and other vegetables in the same pan. You can serve them with meat or fish or on their own with grated cheese.

## Ingredients:

Serves 4

1 lb. small equal-sized
   new potatoes
2 carrots
2 zucchini
2 red onions
2½ tablespoons sunflower,
   vegetable or olive oil
salt and ground black pepper

1. Put a large roasting pan into the oven. Then, preheat the oven to 400°F. Scrub the potatoes clean, then dry them with a paper towel.

2. Peel the carrots with a potato peeler and cut off the ends. Cut the ends off the zucchini, too. Then, cut each zucchini and carrot into about five pieces.

Spoon the vegetables into a dish, if you're serving them at the table.

Cut through the root.

The root holds the onion together as it cooks.

3. Cut the top off the onions. Peel the skin down as far as the root at the bottom, and pull it off. Then, cut each onion into six wedges, from top to bottom.

4. Peel the outer layer of onion off each wedge, as far as the root, and carefully cut it off with a sharp knife. Then, pull any hairy parts off the roots.

5. Put the potatoes into a plastic food bag, then add a tablespoon of olive oil. Hold the bag tightly and shake it, to coat the potatoes all over with oil.

Wear oven mitts – the pan will be very hot.

Turning the vegetables helps them to brown evenly as they cook.

6. Dump the potatoes into a bowl. Put the onion wedges and carrots into the bag and add another tablespoon of oil. Shake the bag, to coat the vegetables.

7. Add the onions and carrots to the bowl. Then, take the hot pan out of the oven and pour the vegetables into it. Spread them out in a single layer.

8. Put the vegetables in the oven and cook them for 15 minutes. Then, wearing oven mitts, carefully lift them out of the oven, and turn them with a spatula.

9. While the vegetables are in the oven, put the pieces of zucchini in the bag with half a tablespoon of oil. Shake the bag, to cover the zucchini pieces with oil.

10. Add the zucchini pieces to the pan and sprinkle all the vegetables with a pinch of salt and of pepper. Then, put them back in the oven for 10 minutes.

11. Take the vegetables out of the oven and turn them again. Then, put them back in the oven for another 10 minutes, or until they are slightly browned.

# Potatoes

Potatoes can be cooked in lots of different ways. On these pages you can find out about different kinds of potatoes, and some of the ways in which you can cook them.

## Four different types

In America, there are four main types of potatoes: russet, long white, round white and round red. The russet is good for baking and frying. Long whites can be baked, boiled or fried. Round white or red potatoes are usually boiled, but are also good for roasting or frying.

## Are they cooked?

Potatoes need to be cooked until they're soft, but different kinds cook at different speeds. To check that they're cooked, push the point of a sharp knife into a potato. If the point goes in easily, it's cooked. If the potato is still a little hard, cook them for a little longer.

New potatoes are not always smooth and round. These thin, knobbed ones are Anya potatoes.

Some new potatoes look clean, but others are really muddy. They need to be gently scrubbed clean.

## Peeling and boiling potatoes

Add a pinch of salt.

1. Rinse the potatoes. To peel each one, hold it in your hand and scrape it with a peeler again and again to remove the skin.

2. If there are spots ('eyes') on the potatoes, cut them out with a sharp knife. Then, cut the potatoes into chunks.

3. Put the potatoes into a pan of cold water. Heat the water until it boils. Reduce the heat so that the water is boiling gently.

4. Put on the lid, leaving a small gap, and cook the potatoes for 20 minutes. Then, carefully drain them through a colander.

These long, thin potatoes are sweet potatoes.

The potato above is a red potato. They are good for baking in their skins.

# New potatoes

Use a clean brush.

Add the potatoes with a spoon.

1. Gently scrub the potatoes. Then, half-fill a pan with water and add a pinch of salt. Heat the water until it boils.

2. Put the potatoes into the pan. Bring them to a boil, then reduce the heat. Boil them for 15-20 minutes, then drain them.

# Baked potatoes

Use a fork to prick the potato several times.

1. Heat your oven to 350°F. Scrub some big baking (russet) potatoes with a soft brush, to remove any dirt.

2. Prick the skins, then bake the potatoes on a baking tray in the oven for 1¼-1½ hours. Check that they are cooked.

# Mashing

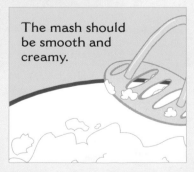

The mash should be smooth and creamy.

Boil long white potatoes, drain them and put them back into the pan, with a little butter, pepper and milk. Mash the potatoes.

# Potato wedges

Cook the wedges until they are golden brown.

1. Preheat the oven to 400°F. Scrub some long white potatoes clean. Cut them in half, then into chunky wedges.

2. Spoon a tablespoon of oil onto a baking tray and add the wedges. Mix them with your hands to lightly coat them with oil.

3. Cook the wedges in the oven for 40-45 minutes. Carefully lift them out and turn them every 15 minutes.

# Fish pie

This pie is a delicious combination of haddock, prawns and green onions, topped with a layer of golden mashed potato. It is best to make it in a fairly deep ovenproof dish.

## Ingredients:

Serves 4

½ fish or vegetable bouillon cube
1 lb. haddock
1½ cups milk
1 bay leaf
salt and ground black pepper
2 lbs. potatoes
8 tablespoons (1 stick) butter
6 green onions
½ cup all-purpose flour
4 oz. cooked peeled prawns, defrosted if frozen
2 tablespoons chopped fresh parsley
1 tablespoon fresh lemon juice

1. Put the bouillon cube into a heatproof container. Then, pour in ½ cup of boiling water and stir it until the bouillon cube has completely dissolved.

2. Put the fish into a pan and pour in the milk and broth. Add the bay leaf and a pinch of salt and of pepper. Heat the mixture on medium heat, until it starts to boil.

The milk mixture will be used to make the sauce.

3. Reduce the heat to low and heat the mixture for five minutes. Then, turn off the heat and lift the fish onto a plate. Carefully pour the milk into a container to cool.

Cook the potatoes while the milk is cooling.

4. Peel the potatoes, cut them into small cubes and put them into the pan. Cover them with cold water and add a pinch of salt. When the milk is cool, remove the bay leaf.

5. Heat the water until it boils, then reduce the heat, so that it is bubbling gently. Put a lid on the pan and cook the potatoes for 15 minutes, or until they are soft.

6. While the potatoes are cooking, break the fish into flakes with a fork. Then, drain the potatoes through a colander and put them back into the pan.

7. Add half of the butter and a pinch of pepper to the potatoes, then mash them until they are smooth. Then, put the rest of the butter into another saucepan.

Use a low heat.

Stir the mixture as it cooks.

Stir the sauce all the time.

8. Cut the ends off the green onions. Remove the outer layer and slice the onions thinly. Then, melt the butter, add the onion slices and cook them for two minutes.

9. Add a spoonful of flour and stir it in. Stir in the rest of the flour, a spoonful at a time. Cook the mixture for one minute, then take the pan off the heat.

10. Add a little "fishy" milk from the container and stir it in. Then, stir in the rest of the milk, a little at a time. Heat the sauce on medium heat, until it boils.

Spoon the fish pie onto four plates and garnish each serving with a sprig of parsley.

Lift out the pie when the top has turned golden.

11. Boil the sauce for one minute, still stirring it, then add the fish, prawns, parsley and lemon juice. Heat the mixture for three more minutes, then take it off the heat.

12. Heat the broiler for five minutes. Spoon the mixture into an ovenproof dish and spoon the potato on top. Cook the pie in the broiler for five minutes.

# Herby roast chicken

In this recipe, lemon and herb butter is pushed under the chicken's skin. The butter melts and adds lemon and herb flavors to the chicken. It also helps to make the meat tender.

## Ingredients:

Serves 4

¼ cup butter, at room
    temperature
3 sprigs of fresh parsley, chopped
1 lemon
salt and ground black pepper
1 onion
1 roasting chicken, about 3½lbs,
    defrosted if frozen
1 bay leaf
1 tablespoon vegetable oil

1. Preheat the oven to 375°F. Put the butter into a small bowl and stir it hard with a wooden spoon, to soften it. Then, add the chopped parsley.

2. Grate the rind of the lemon on the fine holes on a grater, until you have about half a teaspoonful. Add the rind to the butter, then cut the lemon into quarters.

You can cook the chicken with oven-roasted vegetables (see pages 62-63), but you'll need to cook the vegetables for 5-10 minutes longer than it says in the recipe.

Remove any lemon seeds.

3. Squeeze the juice from one lemon quarter into the bowl. Add a large pinch of salt and pepper and mix well. Peel an onion, cut it in half and put it aside.

4. Line a roasting pan with kitchen foil. Then, wash the chicken and put it into the pan. Pat the chicken dry with paper towels. Dry inside the chicken's body, too.

5. Cut out the large piece of fat from inside the chicken. Then, push the onion, the remaining three pieces of lemon and the bay leaf into the cavity in the chicken.

6. Gently push your fingers under the skin over the breast meat, to make a pocket on each side. Then, push the herby butter into the pockets and smooth down the skin.

7. Rub the oil all over the chicken, then wash your hands well. Put the chicken into the oven. After 45 minutes, lift it out carefully, wearing oven mitts.

Use a large metal spoon.

8. Very carefully, tilt the pan, so that the juices run into one end. Then, scoop them up and spoon them over the chicken. This helps to keep the meat moist as it cooks.

9. Put the chicken back into the oven and cook it for another 45 minutes. Check it every so often and if it starts to look dry, lift it out and spoon juices over it again.

10. Push the point of a sharp knife into the meat beside a leg and insert a meat thermometer into the hole. When the temperature reaches 165°F, the chicken is done.

The juices sink back into the meat and make it easier to cut up the chicken.

11. Push a large wooden spoon into the cavity and carefully lift the chicken onto a warm plate. Leave the chicken for 10 minutes, before cutting it into pieces.

# Oven-baked salmon

In this recipe, fillets of salmon are baked in packets made from foil, with thin strips of carrot and leek or green onion. Lemon butter adds a fresh flavor and keeps the fish tender.

## Ingredients:

Serves 4

a leek or 2 green onions
1 carrot
4 tablespoons butter, at room temperature
1 lemon
salt and ground black pepper
4 salmon fillets, each about 5 oz.

1. Preheat the oven to 400°F. While the oven is heating up, cut four 12 inch squares of kitchen foil for the packets and put them to the side for later.

Serve the salmon with boiled new potatoes or mashed potatoes (see pages 64-65).

If you're using a leek, you only need half of it.

2. Cut the leek or onions in half. Cut off the white root and throw it away. Then, cut across one half, to make it into two chunks. Cut the chunks into lots of thin strips.

3. Peel the carrot with a potato peeler, then cut off the ends. Cut the carrot into two or three chunks, then cut them in half, lengthways. Cut the halves into thin strips.

Use the
fine holes
on the
grater.

You'll use the rest of
the juice later on.

4. Put half of the butter into a small bowl and stir it hard with a wooden spoon, until it is soft. Then, grate the rind of the lemon, until you have half a teaspoonful.

5. Cut the lemon in half. Squeeze it on a lemon squeezer, then add a teaspoon of juice, the grated rind and a pinch of salt and of pepper to the butter. Mix everything well.

6. Run your fingers all over each salmon fillet, to feel for any bones that are sticking out. If you find any, pull them out and throw them away.

Don't use
the lemon
butter.

Lay the
fillet with
the skin on
the foil.

7. Using a sharp knife, trim off any fat from the fillets and throw it away. Rinse them under cold water to remove any loose scales, then put the fillets on a clean plate.

8. Using a paper towel, rub the remaining butter over the foil squares, stopping 2 inches away from the edges. Pat the fillets dry with more paper towels.

9. Place one fillet on each square. Sprinkle a teaspoon of lemon juice and strips of carrot and leek or onion over each one. Put small pieces of lemon butter on the top.

10. To make the packets, fold the top and bottom of each foil square over the fillet. Then, pull the sides together and squeeze the foil, to seal the packets.

11. Put the packets onto a baking tray, then bake them in the oven for 15-20 minutes. Then, lift them out and let them cool on the baking tray for five minutes.

12. Open the foil packets very carefully, watching out for the hot steam inside. Lift the fillets out with a spatula, then spoon the vegetables and juices over them.

# One-pot chicken casserole

This Mediterranean-style chicken casserole is a meal all on its own. There is no need to cook extra potatoes or vegetables, as they're already in the casserole.

## Ingredients:

Serves 4

1 lb. (about 4 medium) potatoes

1 chicken or vegetable bouillon cube

1 yellow or red pepper

1 onion

4 skinless, boneless chicken breasts

2 tablespoons vegetable oil

1 clove of garlic

2 teaspoons all-purpose flour

14 oz. can chopped tomatoes

1 teaspoon dried mixed seasoning

salt and ground black pepper

12 pitted black olives

a 2 quart oven-proof casserole dish

Slice each half before you cut it into chunks.

1. Peel the potatoes and cut them in half. Cut each half into 1 inch cubes. Then, put the cubes into a saucepan and pour in cold water until they are covered.

Leave a gap, so that the steam can escape.

2. Heat the water until it boils, then reduce the heat slightly, so that it is bubbling. Put the lid on the pan and cook the potatoes for five minutes, then drain them.

You'll find it easier to serve the casserole if you use a ladle, as there is a lot of sauce.

3. Put the bouillon cube into a heatproof container. Pour in 1 cup of boiling water and stir it until the cube has dissolved. Put the potatoes and broth to the side.

Throw away the pieces of fat.

Cook the chicken until it is lightly browned.

4. Cut the ends off the pepper and remove the seeds. Cut the pepper into thick slices. Then, cut off the ends of the onion and peel it. Cut it in half, slice it and chop it finely.

5. Cut any pieces of white fat off the chicken breasts and cut each one into three or four pieces. Wash your hands well. Then, preheat the oven to 325°F.

6. Put one tablespoon of oil into a large non-stick frying pan and heat it on medium heat for about 30 seconds. Carefully add the chicken and cook it for about 5-6 minutes.

7. Spoon the chicken into a casserole dish. Put the onion and the remaining oil into the frying pan. Peel and crush the garlic and add it, then cook them for 7-8 minutes.

8. Take the pan off the heat, then sprinkle the flour over the top of the onion mixture. Stir it in well, then add a little broth. Stir well, then add some more broth.

9. Stir in the rest of the broth, a little at a time, then put the frying pan back on the heat. Heat it until the broth boils, stirring all the time. Then, take it off the heat.

10. Spoon everything in the pan, including any liquid, into the casserole dish. Then, add the chopped tomatoes, seasoning and two pinches of salt and of pepper.

11. Add the yellow pepper and the potatoes, then stir everything well. Put the lid on the casserole, then put it in the oven for 1¼ hours. Drain the olives through a sieve.

12. After 1¼ hours, take the casserole dish out of the oven and stir in the olives. Then, cook the casserole for another 10 minutes, or until everything is cooked.

# Bread

These pages show you how to make bread dough into rolls, but the same recipe can be used to make a pizza crust (see pages 28-29). You need to give yourself plenty of time to make the dough, because you need to leave it to rise.

## Flour power

Bread is made with special flour called 'bread flour' and yeast. Gentle heat makes the yeast rise, which makes the dough grow. To make the yeast rise, you'll need to leave the dough in a warm place, like an airing cupboard or a warm kitchen.

## Bread rolls

Ingredients:

Makes 12 rolls

3½ cups strong white
   bread flour
a teaspoon of salt
2 teaspoons dried
   rapid rise yeast
   (1 package)
2 teaspoons sugar
1 cup warm water
2 tablespoons olive or
   vegetable oil

Make the hollow in the middle.

1. Sift the flour and the salt into a large mixing bowl, through a sieve. Then, add the yeast and sugar and stir them in.

2. Make a hollow in the flour. Pour the warm water into a container and add the oil, then pour them into the hollow.

3. Stir everything with a wooden spoon, to make a soft dough. Then, dust a clean work surface with flour.

To make a floury bread roll, brush the uncooked roll with milk, then sift plain flour over it, through a sieve.

4. Put the dough on the work surface and knead it for 10 minutes (see opposite). Then, put it into a clean bowl.

5. Cover the bowl with plastic foodwrap. Leave it in a warm place for 1½ hours, until the dough rises to twice its original size.

These rolls were sprinkled with poppy, sesame or sunflower seeds, or rolled oats, after they were brushed with milk.

6. Put the dough back on the floury surface and knead it again, for about a minute, to squeeze out any air bubbles.

Grease the baking tray with oil.

7. Break the dough into 12 pieces. Roll them into balls and put them on a greased baking tray, with spaces between them.

8. Leave the rolls to rise in a warm place for about 40 minutes. Meanwhile, preheat your oven to 425°F.

9. Lightly brush the rolls with milk. Bake them for 12-15 minutes, then lift them out and put them on a wire rack to cool.

## Kneading

1. Press the heels of both hands, or your knuckles, into the dough. Then, push the dough away from you firmly.

2. Fold the dough in half and turn it around. Push the dough away from you again. Then, fold it in half and turn it around.

3. Continue pushing the dough away from you, folding and turning it around, until it feels smooth and springy.

## Herby rolls

For herby rolls, stir two teaspoons of mixed herbs into the flour and salt in step 1 of the main recipe. Then, follow the steps.

# Creamy raspberry ice cream

This delicious ice cream contains crushed raspberries and meringues. You can either use ready-made meringues or make your own (see pages 82-83). Make the ice cream the day before you eat it, because it takes a long time to freeze.

It's not good to re-freeze ice cream when it's been out of the freezer for a while, so put it into two containers if you're not going to eat it all at once.

## Ingredients:

Serves 8

8 oz. (about 70) fresh raspberries
½ cup powdered sugar
½ cup vanilla yogurt
1 cup (½ pint) whipping cream
2 oz. (about 11) meringues

1. Put the raspberries in a colander. Rinse them, then dry them with a paper towel. Put them into a bowl and mash them with a fork until they are fairly smooth.

2. Using a sieve, sift the powdered sugar into the bowl. Stir it into the mashed raspberries. Then, add the yogurt to the mixture and stir everything together well.

3. Pour the cream into a large bowl. Whisk it until it is thick and there are points when you lift the whisk. Then, add the raspberry and yogurt mixture to it.

*If you're eating all the ice cream at once, use one container.*

4. Gently turn the mixture over and over with a spoon, to mix everything together. Then, pour it into two freezer-proof containers and put on the lids.

Decorate each serving of ice cream with a raspberry and a sprig of fresh mint.

5. Put the containers into a freezer for two hours, or until the ice cream is mushy and half-frozen. Meanwhile, break the meringues into small pieces.

6. Quickly mash the ice cream with a fork, to break up any ice crystals. Then, add half of the broken meringues to each container, and stir them in.

7. Put the ice cream back into the freezer for four hours, or until it is firm. Take it out about 15 minutes before you want to eat it, so that it can soften a little.

## Chef's Tip

You'll find it much easier to serve the ice cream if you use a hot spoon or ice cream scoop. Dip the spoon into a mug or bowl of hot water, dry it, then use it.

# Fluffy lemon cheesecake

This light, fluffy cheesecake is easy to make and doesn't need cooking. It does need to chill in the refrigerator for at least four hours, though, so you'll need to make it well before you want to eat it.

## Ingredients:

Serves 6

6 oz. graham crackers
2 tablespoons butter
2 lemons
2½ teaspoons powdered gelatin (not suitable for vegetarians)
8 oz. package regular cream cheese
½ cup plain yogurt
2/3 cup sugar
½ cup whipping cream

8 inch flan pan, or spring-clip pan with a loose base, about 2 inches deep

1. Pour a little cooking oil into the pan and wipe it over the inside of the pan with a paper towel. Then, put the graham crackers into a clean plastic food bag.

2. Put the bag inside another bag and twist a rubber band around the top. Then, roll a rolling pin over the graham crackers, to crush them into crumbs.

3. Put the butter into a saucepan and heat it on low heat until it has melted. Lift the pan off the heat and stir in the cracker crumbs. Mix them in really well.

4. Spoon the mixture into the pan and spread it out. Press it down with the back of a spoon, to make a firm, flat crust. Then, put the pan in the refrigerator.

Cut the cheesecake into slices and decorate each slice with grated lemon rind and a strawberry.

Put the grated rind
to the side.

Be careful not to
splash yourself with
the hot water.

5. Grate the rind of the lemons on the fine holes on a grater. Then, cut the lemons in half and squeeze the juice from them, using a lemon squeezer.

6. Pour five tablespoons of lemon juice and two tablespoons of cold water into a heatproof container. Sprinkle the gelatin over the top and leave it for five minutes.

7. Meanwhile, fill a saucepan with water until it is about 2 inches deep. Heat the water until it boils, then take it off the heat. Carefully put the container into it.

## Chef's Tip

Don't
boil the
gelatin.

In the next step, you need to dissolve the gelatin. Stir the liquid until the grains have dissolved, then lift up a spoonful of the liquid and check that it is clear.

8. When the gelatin has dissolved completely, put on oven mitts and carefully lift the container out of the water. Leave the liquid for five minutes, to cool.

9. Put the cream cheese, yogurt, sugar and lemon rind into a bowl. Stir them hard until the mixture is smooth. Then, pour the cream into another bowl.

Spread out the
mixture with the
back of a spoon.

10. Whisk the cream firmly with a whisk until it is thick. Then, add the cooled gelatin mixture to the cheese mixture and mix it in really well.

11. Add the cream. Then, gently slice through the middle of the mixture with a metal spoon and turn it over. Repeat this until everything is mixed.

12. Pour the mixture into the pan, then put it in the refrigerator for at least four hours, to set. Remove the cheesecake from the pan before serving it.

# Apple crumble

This tasty apple crumble is made with eating apples and can be eaten hot or cold. It is delicious served with a scoop of vanilla ice cream.

## Ingredients:

Serves 4

For the crumble topping:
2/3 cup all-purpose flour
2/3 cup whole-wheat flour
small pinch of ground cinnamon
1 stick (½ cup) butter
¼ cup brown sugar

For the apple filling:
1½ lbs. eating apples
1/8 cup sugar
3 tablespoons orange juice

1. Preheat the oven to 350°F. While it is heating up, sift both kinds of flour and the cinnamon through a sieve into a large bowl, to get rid of any lumps.

2. Pour any bits of bran left in the sieve into the bowl as well. Then, cut the butter into small cubes. Add the cubes to the flour mixture and stir them in.

3. Rub the butter into the flour with the tips of your fingers. Continue until the mixture looks like fine breadcrumbs. Then, stir in the brown sugar.

Throw the core and peel away.

4. On a cutting board, carefully cut each apple in half. Place the halves on the chopping board with their flat side facing down, then cut them in half in again.

5. Using a potato peeler, peel the quarters. Carefully cut the core out of each one, cutting away from you. Then, cut the quarters into small chunks.

6. Put the chunks of apple into a bowl and sprinkle the sugar over them. Using a spoon, mix the apple and sugar together until the apple chunks are covered in sugar.

## Chef's Tip

7. Spoon the apple into a small ovenproof dish and drizzle the orange juice over the top. Spoon the crumble topping over the apple and spread it out evenly.

8. Put the dish onto a baking tray. Put the tray into the oven for 35 minutes, or until the top is lightly browned. Lift out the crumble and let it cool for five minutes.

When you take the crumble out of the oven, you need to check that the apple is cooked. Push the tip of a knife into it. If it isn't soft, cook it for a little longer.

# Mini meringue nests

These meringue nests can be made a day or two before you want to eat them. Just keep them in an airtight container, then fill them with cream and fruit.

## Ingredients:

Makes 8 meringue nests

For the meringues:
2 medium eggs, at room temperature
7 tablespoons sugar

For the filling:
½ cup (¼ pint) heavy cream
½ teaspoon of vanilla
1 tablespoon sugar
8 oz. berries, such as strawberries, raspberries and blueberries

Use non-stick cooking spray, if you prefer.

Cut out the rectangles just inside your pencil lines.

1. Preheat the oven to 225°F. Then, lay two baking trays on baking parchment. Draw around them. Cut out the shapes and lay them in the baking trays.

2. To separate the egg white from the yolk, break one egg on the edge of a bowl. Slide the egg slowly onto a small plate. Then, put an cup over the yolk.

These nests are shown slightly bigger than real size.

You don't use the yolks in this recipe.

3. Holding the cup, tip the plate over the bowl, so that the egg white dribbles into it. Then, do the same with the other egg, so that both whites are in the bowl.

4. Whisk the egg whites with a whisk until they are really thick. When you lift the whisk up, the egg whites should make stiff peaks, like this.

5. Add a heaped teaspoon of sugar to the egg whites. Whisk it in well. Then, keep adding spoonfuls of sugar and whisking them in, until you have added all the sugar.

Put four nests on each tray.

The baking trays will still be hot.

6. To make the nests, scoop up a spoonful of the meringue mixture with a dessertspoon. Then, using a teaspoon, push the spoonful off onto one of the baking trays.

7. Using the back of the teaspoon, make a shallow hollow in the middle of the meringue mixture. Then, make seven more nests, leaving spaces between them.

8. Put the nests in the oven. Bake them for 40 minutes, then turn off the oven, leaving them inside. After 15 minutes, carefully lift them out and let them cool a little.

Spread the cream with a blunt knife.

9. When the nests are cool enough to handle, lift them off the paper. Pour the cream, vanilla and sugar into a small bowl. Strongly whisk them, until the mixture is thick.

10. Wash the berries and dry them with paper towels. Then, when the nests are cold, fill the hollow in each one with cream and decorate them with berries.

# Chocolatey baked bananas

These yummy bananas are baked in foil packets in the oven. Eat the bananas with the hot glossy chocolate sauce drizzled over the top. They are delicious served with ice cream, too.

## Ingredients:

Serves 4

2 tablespoons butter, softened
2 tablespoons brown sugar
1 teaspoon corn syrup
a small pinch of ground
   cinnamon
4 large, firm bananas
1 tablespoon fresh lemon juice

For the chocolate sauce:
½ cup (4 oz.) semi-sweet or
   milk chocolate chips
2 tablespoons corn syrup
1 tablespoon butter
2 tablespoons water

## Chef's Tip

In this recipe, you use corn syrup, which can be tricky to measure. Heat the spoon in hot water before you start, as this makes the syrup slide off easily.

1. Preheat the oven to 400°F. Then, cut four rectangles of kitchen foil for the foil packets. They should each measure about 8 x 12 inches.

Place the bananas lengthways.

3. Peel the bananas and cut each one in half, lengthways. Rub them all over with the lemon juice. Then, place half a banana in the middle of each foil rectangle.

5. To make a packet, fold the short edges of the foil over the banana. Then, pull the long edges together over the top. Squeeze the foil, to seal the packets.

2. Put the butter in a bowl and stir it firmly with a wooden spoon until it is soft and creamy. Then, stir in the sugar, syrup and cinnamon really well, too.

4. Spoon the butter and cinnamon mixture onto the flat sides of the bananas. Then, press the other banana halves on top, to sandwich the mixture in the middle.

6. Put the packets on a baking tray and bake them in the oven for 10 minutes, until the bananas are tender. While they're cooking, make the chocolate sauce.

7. Put the chocolate, syrup, butter and water in a small saucepan. Heat the mixture on low heat and stir it all the time, until it is smooth. Take the pan off the heat.

8. Remove the foil packets from the oven and leave them for about five minutes, to cool. Carefully open the packets, watching out for any hot steam.

9. Carefully tip each packet, so that the bananas and sauce slide into a bowl. Then, use a smaller spoon to drizzle chocolate sauce over the bananas.

# Crêpes

These are a thin kind of pancake called a crêpe. Serve them with syrup, fresh fruit, preserves, honey or chocolate spread.

## Ingredients:

Serves 4 (about 8 crêpes)

For the crêpes:
1 cup all-purpose flour
salt
1 medium egg
1 cup milk
sunflower oil, for greasing

Suggested toppings:
pancake syrup, chocolate sauce and powdered sugar, fresh fruit or fruit preserves

1. Put the flour and a pinch of salt into a sieve and sift them into a large bowl. Make a deep hollow in the middle of the flour. Then, break the egg into a cup.

2. Pour the egg into the hollow, then start to mix it with a whisk. Meanwhile, add a little milk and gradually mix the milk and egg with the flour around the hollow.

Fold the crêpes into quarters, then pile them up and drizzle them with syrup.

3. Add some more milk and mix it with more of the flour. Repeat this until all the ingredients are mixed together. Then, whisk the batter well, to mix in any lumps.

4. Pour a little of the oil into a cup, ready for greasing the pan. Then, heat a 8-9 inch non-stick frying pan on medium heat for about a minute.

5. Dip a paper towel into the oil and carefully wipe the inside of the pan with it. Be very careful that your fingers don't touch the hot pan.

The batter will bubble as it cooks.

6. Pour about half a ladleful of batter into the pan, then take the pan off the heat immediately. Carefully swirl the batter around, to spread it out into a circle.

7. Put the pan back on the heat and cook the crêpe for about a minute, until the top looks dry. Loosen the edges with a spatula and check that it is golden brown.

8. Slide the spatula under the crêpe, then lift the crêpe and turn it over. Cook it for another 30 seconds, then slide it out of the pan, onto a plate.

## Chef's Tip

9. Cover the crêpe with a clean dish towel, to keep it warm. Then, heat the pan and wipe on more oil. Make more crêpes, until all the batter is finished.

When you're making crêpes, the first one often doesn't work very well. If this happens, don't worry – throw it away and just make some more.

87

# Strawberry shortcake

This strawberry shortcake is made from layers of sweet biscuit, cream and strawberries. Put the layers together just before you want to eat it.

## Ingredients:

Serves 8

For the shortcake:
2 cups self-rising flour
1 teaspoon baking powder
4 tablespoons butter or margarine
2 tablespoons sugar
1 medium egg
4 tablespoons milk
½ teaspoon vanilla
extra milk, for brushing

For the filling:
8 oz. strawberries
½ cup (¼ pint) whipping cream
2 tablespoons sugar
3 tablespoons plain yogurt
powdered sugar

Use a sieve.

1. Preheat the oven to 425°F. Using a paper towel, wipe some butter over a baking tray. Then, sift the flour and baking powder into a large bowl.

2. Cut the butter into small cubes. Add the cubes to the flour, then rub them in with the tips of your fingers. Continue until the mixture looks like fine breadcrumbs.

Decorate the top of the shortcake with half strawberries.

3. Stir in the sugar and make a hollow in the middle of the mixture with a spoon. Then, break the egg into a cup and stir it with a fork, to mix the white and yolk.

4. Stir the milk and vanilla into the egg, then pour the mixture into the hollow in the flour. Mix all the ingredients with a blunt knife, to make a soft dough.

5. Sprinkle a clean work surface with a little flour, then shape the dough into a ball with your hands. Squash the ball a little, then put it onto the work surface.

Remove the stalks before you slice the strawberries.

Cut the shortcake like this.

6. Using a rolling pin, roll out the dough until it is a circle which is about 8 inches across. Lift the dough onto the baking tray and brush it with a little milk.

7. Bake the shortcake in the oven for 12-15 minutes, until it has risen and is golden brown. Meanwhile, rinse and dry the strawberries, then cut them into thick slices.

8. Take the shortcake out of the oven and slide it onto a wire rack, to cool. When the shortcake is cool, very carefully cut it into two layers with a bread knife.

Put the shortcake on a plate.

9. Lift the top layer onto a cutting board and cut it into eight wedges. Then, pour the cream and sugar into a bowl and whisk the mixture until it is thick. Mix in the yogurt.

10. Using a blunt knife, spread half of the mixture over the bottom half of the shortbread. Then, lay the strawberry slices all over the top of the mixture.

11. Spread the rest of the cream mixture over the strawberries. Lay the eight shortcake wedges on the top, then sift powdered sugar over the top of the shortcake.

# Raspberry cream puffs

These pastry puffs are stuffed with raspberry cream. They are best served with hot chocolate sauce poured all over them.

## Ingredients:

Serves 4-6

For the pastry puffs:
2 medium eggs
½ cup all-purpose flour
4 tablespoons butter
½ cup water

For the raspberry cream:
5 oz. (40-50) fresh raspberries
2 tablespoons sugar
½ cup whipping cream

For the chocolate sauce:
½ cup (4 oz.) semi-sweet or
   milk chocolate chips
2 tablespoons corn syrup
1 tablespoon butter
2 tablespoons water

Shake off the water.

1. Preheat the oven to 400°F. Using paper towels, wipe some butter over two baking trays. Hold each baking tray under cold water for a few seconds.

2. Sift the flour through a sieve onto a piece of greaseproof paper. Then, break the eggs into a small bowl and beat them with a fork, to mix the whites and yolks.

You could pile all the puffs in a heap, before pouring on the chocolate sauce.

3. Cut the butter into small pieces and put it into a saucepan with the water. Heat the pan very gently on low heat. As soon as the mixture boils, take it off the heat.

4. Immediately, pour all the flour into the pan. Stir it in for about a minute, until the mixture begins to form a ball in the middle of the pan. Let it cool for five minutes.

5. Add a little egg. Stir it in hard, then repeat this until you've added all the egg. Then, put teaspoonfuls of dough onto the baking trays, leaving spaces in between them.

6. Bake the puffs for 10 minutes, then turn up the heat to 425°F. Bake the puffs for another 10-15 minutes, until they are puffy and dark golden.

7. Lift the baking trays out of the oven and put the puffs onto a wire rack, using a spatula. Then, prick a hole in the side of each one with a sharp knife, to let out any steam.

8. Put the raspberries in a colander and rinse them. Dry them with paper towels, then put them into a bowl with the sugar. Mash them with a fork until they are smooth.

9. Pour the cream into a bowl and beat it with a whisk until it is thick and there are points when you lift the whisk. Then, add the mashed raspberries and mix them in.

10. When the puffs are completely cold, cut a hole in the side of each one. Using a teaspoon, fill the hollow inside them with the raspberry cream mixture.

11. Put the puffs into bowls. Put them in the refrigerator, then make the chocolate sauce, following step 7 on page 85. Pour the sauce over the puffs and serve them.

# Sticky chocolate cake

This sponge cake is made by mixing all the ingredients in the same bowl. It is covered in a layer of sticky chocolate icing and has some of the chocolate in the middle, too. It's delicious on its own or with cream poured over it.

## Ingredients:

Makes about 8 slices

For the sticky chocolate icing:
5 oz. milk chocolate (bar or chips)
¾ cup heavy cream

For the chocolate sponge cake:
1½ cups self-rising flour
½ teaspoon baking powder
4 tablespoons cocoa powder
6 medium eggs
1 cup margarine, softened
2 tablespoons and 1 cup
   brown sugar
1 tablespoon milk

two 8 inch round cake pans

## Chef's Tip

When you're making a cake, take the eggs and margarine out of the refrigerator half an hour before you start. This makes the ingredients easier to mix.

1. For the chocolate icing, break the chocolate into pieces. Put the pieces into a heatproof bowl and add the cream. Then, pour about 2 inches water into a saucepan.

The cold makes the chocolate thicken.

3. Let the icing cool for a few minutes. Then, put it in the refrigerator for at least an hour, stirring it every now and then. Meanwhile, make the cake.

Use non-stick cooking spray, if you prefer.

Cut out the circles just inside your pencil lines.

5. Draw around the pans, cut out the circles and put them into the pans. Then, put the flour, baking powder and cocoa into a sieve and sift them into a large bowl.

2. Heat the water until it bubbles, then take the pan off the heat. Put the bowl into the pan and stir the chocolate and cream until the chocolate has melted.

4. Preheat the oven to 350°F. Pour a little cooking oil into each pan and wipe it over the insides with a paper towel. Then, put the pans on some greaseproof paper.

Stir the mixture until it is smooth.

6. Break the eggs into a cup. Add them to the large bowl, then add the margarine, sugar and milk. Stir everything well. Spoon the mixture into the pans and smooth the tops.

If the cakes are cooked, they will spring back when pressed.

This loosens the edges, making the cakes easier to turn out.

Use a blunt knife.

7. Bake the cakes in the oven for about 25 minutes. Then, wearing oven mitts, carefully lift them out. Press them with a finger, to see if they are cooked.

8. Leave the cakes in the pans for five minutes. Run a knife around them and turn them out onto a wire rack. Peel off the greaseproof paper and leave them to cool.

9. Spread some of the icing over the top of one of the cakes, then put the other cake on top. Then, spread the rest of the icing over the outside of the cake.

Keep the cake in a refrigerator until you are ready to eat it.

# Useful cooking tips

There are many simple skills that cooks use all the time, but they're not all obvious when you start cooking.

On this page, there are a few tips and hints which you may find useful:

## Using a food processor

Click the bowl into place.

Make sure that both parts of the lid are in place.

1. When you're using a food processor, always be very careful of the sharp blades. First, put the food into the plastic bowl.

2. Put on the main lid and twist it on firmly. Turn on the food processor and process the food for as long as you need to.

## Whisking cream

The cream gets thicker as air bubbles are whisked in.

1. Pour the cream into a bowl. Hold the bowl tightly in one hand and twist the whisk around and around very quickly.

2. Whisk the cream until it starts to form stiff peaks when you lift the whisk, then stop before it becomes too solid.

## Clean bowls

When you're whisking egg whites, use a clean, dry bowl and whisk. If you don't, the whites won't go light and fluffy.

## Sticky doughs

To stop a dough from sticking to your hands and kitchen equipment, dust your hands and equipment with flour.

## Juicing a lemon

1. If a recipe includes lemon juice, you can use bottled juice, but fresh juice is better. First, cut a lemon in half.

2. To squeeze out the juice, press one half at a time onto a lemon squeezer. Twist the lemon as you press down.

## Grating cheese

1. If you're grating cheese, there's always a little left over, so cut a piece that's a little bigger than you need.

2. Grate some of the cheese, then measure the cheese you have grated. If there isn't enough, grate some more.

## Thickening sauces

1. When you heat sauces, they get thicker, especially if there is flour in them. To keep them from sticking, stir them often.

2. To make a sauce thicker, heat it over a low heat, until it is as thick as you want it to be. Stir it all the time.

# Index

Digital manipulation by Emma Julings and John Russell